A Toast to Love

Books by Barbara Stephens

A TOAST TO LOVE
WAYWARD LOVER

A Toast to Love

BARBARA STEPHENS

DOUBLEDAY & COMPANY, INC.

GARDEN CITY, NEW YORK

1984

All of the characters in this book
are fictitious, and any resemblance
to actual persons, living or dead,
is purely coincidental.

Library of Congress Cataloging in Publication Data
Stephens, Barbara.
A Toast to Love.
I. Title.
PS3569.T3834T6   1984   813′.54
ISBN 0-385-18131-0

Library of Congress Catalog Card Number 82–45339

First Edition

For
my
parents
Oveta and Adolphus

CHAPTER 1

With a fluffy white bath sheet Paige Avalon dried off
swiftly and massaged her body with a creamy musk-
scented lotion that gave her deep bronze complexion a
soft glow. She slipped into lacy beige lingerie and began making up her face, dabbing a bit of translucent
powder to the tip of her fine-drawn nose and highlighting her high cheekbones with dark red rouge. Her large
round thickly lashed eyes were striking, and she accented them delicately with sable-brown and bone-
pearl eyeshadow. She brushed her full lips with clear
red lip gloss and pulled her shoulder-length dark hair
back from her face and knotted it. Thoughtfully, Paige
went to her closet and began pushing through some of
the garments. She wanted to look her best for Steven.
She wanted to wear something memorable for this special night. After considering several dresses hanging
lifelessly from satin-padded hangers, Paige slipped a
simple white long-sleeved shift over her lean frame
instantly enlivening the silk-jersey fabric. She pulled on
silk cream-colored sandals with high thin heels and
stepped in front of a full-length mirror. The pearls, she
thought. Gram's pearls will be the perfect accessory.
Quickly she studded her ears with the huge pale gray
gems and hung a waist-length matching rope of them
around her neck.

Looking at her reflection in the mirror, Paige
thought of her grandmother and smiled. The world

knew her as Andriette Brandon, the great American jazz pianist. In her early twenties, Andriette had moved to Europe where her music rapidly became popular in the elite supper clubs of Berlin, Madrid, Rome and Paris. She captured the hearts of royalty as well as the common man and soon became the toast of the Continent.

After several years abroad, Andriette returned to New York City to visit her parents and was given a hero's welcome. During her stay, she found herself in demand to perform at concerts as well as private social gatherings. Andriette extended her visit and following a successful tour in America became celebrated throughout the world.

When once again she traveled to Europe, the renowned pianist met and married John Luke de Gaulle, a French banker. Three years later, Bridget, their only child, was born. It was in a New York City hospital, more than twenty years later, that Bridget gave birth to her only child, Paige.

Since the day of her granddaughter's birth, Andriette had showered her with lavish gifts. The exquisite jewelry that she gave Paige on her last trip to America was no exception. The pearls she now wore had come from the Orient. A second necklace of rubies, encrusted with diamonds, which lay snug in a small safe in her closet, had been cut and set in South America. Additionally, Andriette had brought her granddaughter furnishings from her houses in Paris and Rome that the young woman had often admired. And during that exciting fall holiday they decorated Paige's spacious tenth-floor Riverside Drive apartment with Persian rugs, antique Italian furniture, expensive oil paintings and scatterings of Steuben glass. It had taken several days for them to set up the apartment to their liking, and afterward, they had celebrated the success of their decorating venture with dinner at the Gaslight, a cozy little restaurant in midtown Manhattan.

"So, what's next on your agenda?" Andriette had asked her granddaughter.

"All I want to do now, Gram, is concentrate on my career," Paige answered.

"Oh? And what does Steven have to say about that? Or are you making plans according to his wishes?"

"Gram!" Paige was shocked. "I'd never allow some man to dictate my life to me."

"I wasn't of the impression that Steven is *some man*," her grandmother had responded. "I thought you had very special feelings for him."

"Well, I do. But that doesn't mean I'll allow him to plan my future based on his hopes and dreams."

"I see."

Puzzled by her grandmother's concerned expression, Paige had attempted to clarify her point of view further. "Gram, you of all people should understand how I feel about my career. It's very important to me."

"Of course I understand. But, does Steven? Some men would resent the woman in their lives having demanding work, such as yours."

"Steven and I have thoroughly discussed his work and mine as well. We know what to expect of each other."

"Good. You're very much your own woman, Paige. You know what you want and you're not afraid to go after it."

"Every one says I'm just like you, Gram. You never allowed anyone to order you about either. Not even Grandpa."

Andriette's laughter had reminded Paige of wind chimes on a sunny spring afternoon. "I know," she said. "And I was called a maverick. I was out of step with my times, Paige."

"But very much in step with mine. Women today are free to have whatever career they like and marriage, too. Men understand and accept that."

"Wonderful. Now, tell me. When do you think you and Steven will marry? I'd hate to be on tour at the time and miss the ceremony." Although Andriette Brandon was well into her eighties, she toured constantly and was still the toast of five continents.

Paige smiled and took her grandmother's hand in hers. "We haven't decided, yet, Gram, but when we do you'll be the first to know."

Only a few months had passed since that conversation and Paige knew before the night ended she would write to her grandmother.

The doorbell chimed softly, jarring her out of her reflective mood. And without delay, Paige crossed the room to the entryway.

Steven Edwards stepped through the door and handed Paige a single long-stemmed red rose. "A gift for my lady," he said. The young engineer was tall and thin and wore a light blue shirt with a navy pinstripe suit that complemented his distinguished good looks.

Paige smiled and kissed him lightly on the lips, and arm in arm they entered the living room. "I've chilled a bottle of champagne," she told him. "Shall I get it?" Suddenly she was nervous. Paige couldn't believe that she was losing her control.

Steven's right eyebrow shot up and a slow smile creased his face. "That's perfect," he said. "This evening does call for a celebration."

Paige slipped the rose into the slim hand-painted porcelain vase that held the buds he always brought her. She poured the sparkling dry wine into fluted crystal goblets and, handing Steven one, sat across from him on the sofa. "Now, I'm all set to hear about this big decision you've made," she said. "You sounded so happy and excited when you telephoned this morning." Appreciatively, Paige fixed him with her large brown eyes. She liked the gray in his dark hair at the temples, his smooth tawny brown complexion and keen even features. He's good-looking, she thought. She would be proud to become Mrs. Steven Edwards.

A self-satisfied smile pulled at his lips as Steven got to his feet and began pacing about the apartment. Paige would be the perfect wife for him, he reasoned. She was elegant, well-educated and had a good family background. Her parents were successful doctors and had spent many years practicing medicine in Africa before opening offices in New York City. Her father's parents had just retired from administrative jobs with the public school system. And of course the world would forever sing the praises of her maternal grandmother, Andriette Brandon. Paige's interesting and varied background had fashioned her into a woman who would be an asset to him or any man. He was lucky to have fallen in love with her.

Steven returned to the sofa and sat beside Paige. After fumbling in his pocket for a moment, he withdrew a small velvet box and handed it to her. "Be my wife, Paige," he said softly.

Paige stared at the expensive case clutched in Steven's long thin fingers before taking it and flipping up its top. A platinum and diamond engagement ring, resting on a white satin pillow, sparkled brilliantly under the light. Slowly, she lifted her lashes and met his gaze. "Oh yes, Steven," she whispered.

Steven slipped the ring on her finger and their lips met in a warm and tender kiss. At long last, after forcing himself to break their embrace, Steven reluctantly released Paige. "I have some more good news," he said. "I've been offered the position of group vice president with the Roll, Hart, and Blair Engineering Company and I've accepted it."

"Oh, Steven, that's wonderful."

"I knew you'd be pleased," he said. "However, it does mean we'll have to rush our wedding plans. We're leaving for the Middle East in two months."

A tiny frown creased Paige's forehead. "Why?" she asked.

"My new position is with the company's branch office there," Steven explained, his face a mirror of happiness. "I'm expected to begin work by July first."

Shaking her head slowly, Paige stared at him, her large eyes empty of expression. "I can't go to the Middle East, Steven."

Her words stunned him. "What do you mean?" he asked.

"I have my career to consider. I could never do my work while living outside America."

"Paige, you'll just have to put your work aside until we return to the States in a few years. My career must come first."

Inwardly Paige shivered as she digested his message. On the day they had met, over a year ago, she had told Steven of her dreams to teach in a small college and establish herself as an American historian with an emphasis on Afro-American life. And since that time she had worked diligently toward that goal. She had clearly

explained to him the work involved and her timetable.
How could he now casually ask her to give up all she
had labored for? Hadn't he been listening to her or did
he simply choose to disregard all her plans? How could
he even suggest that she put her career aside for several
years? "And what will I do all day while you're working?" she asked. "Twiddle my thumbs?"

"No," Steven answered, a little annoyed with her
illogical question. "We'll have to do an awful lot of en-
tertaining and much of your time will be spent caring
for our home and planning dinner parties and the like.
You know, you're a wonderful hostess, Paige."

"Steven, do you realize what you're asking of me?"

"Yes. I'm asking you to become a very important part
of my life."

"And in doing so I'd have to relinquish mine."

"What are you talking about, Paige?"

"My life. I've spent most of it preparing myself to
teach and concentrate on my writing. I didn't earn a
doctor of philosophy degree in history from Columbia
University just to be your hostess, Steven."

"Don't be silly. Being my wife will be a full-time job
in itself. You can utilize all of your skills in that capacity."

"Not really," Paige said, a ripple of anger moving
determinedly through her. Feeling bruised, she toyed
deliberately with the diamond on her finger and
watched the light dance off the polished facets of the
flawless stone. It was the first time she'd ever been so
terribly angry with Steven, but it was also the first time
he'd ever insulted her intelligence. Nevertheless, his
intent had come into clear focus. Steven had never
seriously considered her plans. "I need more," she told
him.

"And, you have more. In a year or two, we'll start our family. Now, won't that be fulfilling enough for you?"

"No." The word hung in the air between them like a child's party balloon filled with helium. She could imagine nothing in the world that could induce her to give up teaching. The security of being a faculty member and the quiet elegance of the intellectual life had long been her dream. Meeting Steven was a pleasant addition, and she saw no reason why she should alter her plans by marrying him. And, she couldn't imagine getting these things overseas. She needed time to reach her goal, and for the moment, she was unwilling to put her work aside to pour her energy into the roles of homemaker, wife and mother. Steven would have to accept that. "I can't go with you now," she said, thoughtfully. "I owe it to myself to at least try to accomplish some of the career objectives I've worked toward for so long. This means so much to me. I'd hate to go through life feeling that I'd never given myself a chance." Abruptly Paige met his gaze as she realized yet another reason why she couldn't go with him. "Besides, the Middle East is dangerous right now. Why don't you turn this position down and wait for another one in a safer area?"

Steven sighed deeply and rearranged himself on the sofa. "This job is the opportunity I've been waiting for, and I'm going to grab it," he said coolly. "Furthermore, I wouldn't go or ask you to go someplace where I felt we might get hurt. I'm confident we'll be as safe there as we are here walking the streets of New York City." He fixed her with a steady gaze. "So, Paige, what's your answer? I want you to be my wife." He picked up his glass from the side table and drank from it.

"Give me a year, Steven. You knew what I wanted to do. It's only fair. After that we can make some plans."

"Are you suggesting a long-distance relationship? An extended engagement?"

"Yes, Steven. I need some time."

He leaned forward, slowly swirling the pale yellow liquid in his glass. His face grew tense with concentration and color drained from his cheeks. In one smooth motion he swallowed the last of his wine and tried to camouflage his swing in mood with a smile. He failed. He got to his feet and began pacing about the apartment, once again. "Time. That's something I don't have, Paige. And I don't believe in long-distance romances. We'll either get married now and you go with me to the Middle East, or forget it."

A cold chill raced down Paige's spine and her thoughts whirled helter-skelter about in her head as she comprehended the meaning of his statements. "We don't have to forget anything, Steven. We've only known each other for a little more than a year. We can afford to wait a year or two before making our wedding plans."

"No, Paige. You'll have to decide now."

"You're being awfully selfish, Steven."

"I don't think so."

"I do. Nevertheless, I love you."

"And I love you."

Recognizing she had lost the battle, Paige slipped the ring from her finger, placed it back in the little velvet box and snapped the lid shut. Slowly, she extended her arm and gave it back to him. Tears sprang to her eyes. Turning down Steven's marriage proposal was the most difficult thing she'd ever done in her life. Her head throbbed. Each strand of hair that made up the knot at the nape of her neck began to pull unmercifully at her scalp. Her skin became warm and damp. A ball formed and tightened in the pit of her stomach. Steven was walking out of her life. He was throwing away the beautiful year and a half they'd shared. The tears spilled from her eyes, rolled down her cheeks and finally found a resting place in the white silk fabric of her dress. It was all so unreal. "I'm sorry you feel that you can't wait, Steven, but if you should ever find that you've changed your mind, please let me know."

"I won't change my mind, Paige," he said, slipping the case into his pocket. "And I'm sorry, too."

Paige watched as the man she loved walked unceremoniously out of her life. Steven moved quickly across the room and out of the door.

Paige made her way up several flights of stairs and to the office of Dr. Carlton Blake at Columbia University. She knocked softly on the frame of his door and waited to be acknowledged. As her large brown eyes swept the office cluttered with books and papers, warm memories of past visits with the staid old history professor flooded her mind.

She had spent many long evenings with him there in his small office discussing American history, current events, her future and his life's work. And over the years they grew to be close friends. Paige treasured their time together, for she realized she learned more from those sessions than she did in most of her classes. Seeing him at this time made her aware of how much she had missed him.

The old man carefully closed the notebook he was writing in and peered over his bifocals at her standing in the doorway. "Oh, Dr. Avalon," he said in a low gravelly voice, "come in and have a seat." She stepped into the room permeated with the poignant familiar smell of pipe tobacco and sat in a well-worn brown leather chair. With patience she watched the stocky, white-haired professor remove his glasses, wipe the lenses purposefully with a tissue and readjust the wire frames on his nose. "I've been trying to reach you for several weeks, now," he told her. "Finally, I gave up on Ma Bell and decided to try the postal system. It worked." He chuckled with self-satisfaction.

A wave of anxiety rushed through Paige. What was so important that Carlton Blake had summoned her to his office? Eight months had passed since she received her degree.

"I've been very busy lately, Dr. Blake." She almost laughed at her understatement inasmuch as the past few months of her life had been spent in a maelstrom of activity. Her breakup with Steven had left her deeply depressed, and for weeks she had struggled to push the memory of him out of her consciousness. From work she raced to exercise class, the theater or a concert. Weekends were spent with friends in antique shops, museums, art galleries, parties and church. She cycled through Central Park or jogged around the reservoir. And at long last the tears that had been her constant companion ceased, leaving behind the persistent pain that threatened to consume her being. But that too had begun to fade, and Paige was once again adhering to a more reasonable schedule. More important, she had successfully put to rest many of the doubts and fears that had plagued her since Steven walked out of her life. Paige no longer felt herself a failure, but instead a survivor. A winner.

". . . a letter from my friend Nathan Buchanan in

Texas, and he's looking for an instructor for his department at Huston-Tillotson College."

"What . . . What did you say?"

The old professor got to his feet and began pacing the small area between his desk and her chair. His lightweight baggy suit was the same faded gray color as his small piercing eyes, and with the precision of a marching soldier he measured his steps as he walked. Momentarily he paused, toyed with the clay pipe held tightly between his teeth and gazed at Paige. "What's the matter, Dr. Avalon? Have you developed a hearing problem since last I saw you?"

She smiled with embarrassment. "I'm sorry. My thoughts strayed for a moment. Did you mention Dr. Buchanan?"

"Yes, I did." He resumed his pacing and Paige watched his measured steps. "You told me once you wanted to teach in a small college and do research in the area of black American life. This seems to be the perfect opportunity for you. Nathan is looking for an instructor and research assistant."

Paige could scarcely believe the chance Dr. Blake was offering her. She had been an admirer of Nathan Buchanan, the celebrated historian, since childhood. His teaching career, sixteen books and numerous articles had served as inspiration and example for the career she planned for herself. "The position sounds perfect in every way, Dr. Blake. How can I ever repay you for thinking of me?"

Carlton Blake ceased his pacing and returned to the chair behind his massive old wooden desk. "I know you'll do your best, Paige," he answered softly. "That's all the payment I require. Now, Nathan would like to have you in Texas by the first of next month. Can you make arrangements to be there?"

Next month. May. Her birth month. She was being given the opportunity to begin her twenty-seventh year with new hopes and dreams. Not only would she have the good fortune to lay the foundation of her career under the tutelage of the esteemed Nathan Buchanan, but the move would also help expedite her efforts to get over Steven Edwards. Paige wanted to burst into songs of joy and dance about the room, but she knew the proper old history professor would have been horrified by such a blatant display of emotion. And so, instead, she remained in her chair feigning composure. "Yes, I can," she answered.

CHAPTER 2

Magda Winslow, an attractive middle-aged woman with a Castilian brown complexion and short auburn hair, skillfully maneuvered a black Lincoln sedan through the rolling terrain of the Texas hill country. With sparkling almond-shaped eyes, she periodically glanced at Paige sitting in the passenger seat next to her. "Nathan is anxious to meet you, Dr. Avalon," she said, "and was pleased you agreed to come to his home in Greens Cove for lunch." A look of concern crossed her features. "He hated the idea of you spending your first day in Austin alone."

"That was kind of him," Paige replied. "I can't think of anything I'd like better than to spend the afternoon visiting with Dr. Buchanan. Do you work with him at the college?"

"Oh no, dear. I don't teach at Huston-Tillotson. I'm what you may call Nathan's handywoman. Among other things, I'm his secretary and chauffeur."

"Your job sounds interesting, Miss Winslow," Paige said.

"It is, my dear," Magda replied. "It is."

Less than a year had passed since Magda Winslow and Nathan Buchanan had met on a Caribbean cruise. They had been seated at the same table for dinner their first night at sea and found themselves quite compatible. Subsequently, they spent their holiday together, swimming, dancing and strolling in the moonlight.

And, one month later, when the ship returned to port in Florida, and for the first time in her life Magda Winslow found herself in love.

Prior to that time, she had chosen not to marry and had enjoyed a happy and productive life. But after her holiday at sea, her needs had changed. She loved Nathan and wanted with all her heart to be his wife.

Knowing Nathan shared her feelings, Magda immediately marked out a course that would keep her near him. She took an early retirement from her job in Houston as legal secretary at Taylor and Jones law firm where she had worked since graduation from college thirty years before. She then moved to Austin and talked the historian into hiring her as his private secretary, gradually assuming responsibility for much of his personal affairs. And, after several weeks of daily driving out to Greens Cove from the city, Magda finally convinced Nathan that she should move into the small apartment adjoining his home since she now had the duty of running his household. The arrangement had worked out beautifully and according to her plans. During that short period their love had grown and Magda had felt certain Nathan was about to ask her to be his wife. But that had changed. Something terrible had happened to him and now he was trying to push her out of his life.

After a twenty-minute drive out of the city they turned onto a private winding cobbled road that rose and dipped with the hills and valleys it traversed. And a quarter of a mile later Magda brought the sedan to a stop in front of a garage located several yards behind a three-story Queen Anne-style white house trimmed with navy blue.

"This way," she said, getting out of the car and leading the way. They followed a flagstone walk across the lawn and around the mansion to the gray-painted porch where Nathan Buchanan waited for them.

Paige's breath caught in her throat as she watched the man she'd never dreamed she'd be fortunate enough to meet get to his feet and walk briskly toward them. A winsome smile creased his handsome face. She was surprised to see that he looked at least a decade younger than his seventy years. He was tall, well over six feet, lean and regal. His smooth brown skin had been kissed by the sun, giving his complexion a rosy glow. Closely trimmed silver-gray hair and a thin mustache accented his even, bold features. He wore perfectly tailored beige gabardine slacks and a short-sleeved shirt of fine white cotton, which called attention to his large, firm arms. "It was kind of you to come on such short notice," he said, his voice deep and vibrant. His dark eyes twinkled with kindness as he took Paige's hand in his.

"I'm thrilled to be here, Dr. Buchanan," she replied softly.

The stately old gentleman threw up his hands as if to silence her. "Not so formal, young lady," he chided gently. "My faculty members call me Nat and I expect you to do the same."

"Of course," Paige agreed with a nervous laugh, wondering all the while how she would ever bring herself to call the distinguished historian by a shortened version of his first name.

"I'll get some cool drinks and your lunch," Magda said, going into the house. "You can eat out here."

"We'd like that," Nathan told her. He led Paige to the curved corner of the Victorian wraparound porch where they sat at a white-eyelet-skirted table under a conical roof. "My friend, Carlton Blake, tells me you're quite a capable and ambitious young woman," he said, studying Paige closely. "I'm proud you've accepted my offer to become a part of our faculty here at Huston-Tillotson."

"Never in my wildest dreams did I think I'd ever have the privilege to work under your guidance, Nat," Paige said. "Thank you for giving me such a wonderful opportunity."

Dr. Buchanan smiled. "The privilege is mine," he replied, "and I hope Huston-Tillotson and I can live up to your expectations." Magda brought out tall glasses filled with iced tea and chicken salads arranged on crisp green lettuce leaves. "Aha, Magda," Nathan said, assisting her with the tray, "this looks delicious. Thank you."

A cool breeze rustled the branches of the lovely old oak trees growing around the porch and lawn while they had their lunch. "We live outside almost year round," Dr. Buchanan told Paige. "You're going to find life in Texas very different from what you're used to in New York City."

"I'm looking forward to it."

"Oh? You sound happy to have left the East Coast."

"I am," Paige said. "I needed a change."

"I see. And what about your job at New York University? Are you happy to have left it, also?"

"I enjoyed my work there, Nat, but my dream has always been to teach at a small college."

"Good," he smiled, satisfied with her answers. Watching Paige finish her salad, he asked, "Would you like something more?"

"No. That was plenty."

He got to his feet and offered her his arm. "Come and stretch your legs," he said.

They walked the length of the porch that was comfortably and completely equipped as an outdoor living room with lacy white wicker furniture and a pastel-colored cotton rug. She followed him down several steps to the lawn where they took a footpath bordered with colorful spring flowers and lush green shrubbery to a huge pond.

"It's lovely here," Paige told him, looking beyond the still water at the rolling green hills in the distance. "It's so peaceful and beautiful."

"This place holds many happy memories for me," Dr. Buchanan replied thoughtfully. "My grandparents built this house before the turn of the century. My parents were married in the parlor, and my brother, Philip, and I were born in the west upstairs bedroom." He laughed softly. "As you can see, many of the important events of my family occurred right on this land. Philip and I spent our childhoods here. Those years were some of the happiest of my life. A thousand acres of land can hold quite a bit of fascination for two little boys." He winked at Paige and smiled. "I think we must have explored every inch of it at least twice."

"What a wonderful way to grow up," Paige said.

"Yes," Dr. Buchanan confirmed. "We were fortunate."

Though Nathan Buchanan spent his youth in the Texas hill country, he lived his later years, after earning his doctorate from Yale University, far from his southwestern birthplace. He met and married his wife, Mary Ann, while living in Connecticut, and together they worked and traveled throughout Europe, Africa, South America, Mexico and several states in the North American Deep South. During that time he taught and lectured at various colleges and universities and wrote sixteen books and innumerable articles on black life in the Western World.

Mary Ann died while they were working in Mexico. Nathan then returned to his native Texas, where a few months later he witnessed the untimely death of his brother in a hunting accident. Nevertheless, after six years and with courage and determination, Nathan had at last succeeded in building a new life for himself.

"Do you have children?" Paige asked.

For a moment Dr. Buchanan looked forlorn. "No," he answered. "Mary Ann and I were never blessed with children. But I do have a wonderful nephew, Kyle, who lives in Houston. He's a great joy and comfort to me."

They made their way back to the porch and took seats on a sofa, which had sea-blue-and-white-striped pillows. Dr. Buchanan picked up a pair of binoculars that lay on the end table next to him. After gazing through them for a second, he quickly handed the glasses to Paige. "Look at my friend, there," he said, gesturing.

Paige adjusted the lenses and aimed the binoculars in the direction of his pointing finger. High in a spreading oak tree, a small gray squirrel happily scampered along an outstretched branch. Periodically he stopped to look about him and listen to the messages in the wind. "Is he tame?" she asked.

"Not completely," Dr. Buchanan replied, "but often he'll take food from my hands. Many of the small animals will. I call them all my friends and keep an eye on my little comrades from time to time with these." He indicated the binoculars. "My wife used to collect binoculars, and when I moved back here I began watching mother nature, the animals and the weather, through them. I keep a pair in almost every room of the house.

Once I even watched a tornado bounce about the fields there in the distance."

"Nathan, you have a telephone call," Magda said, sticking her head out of the front door.

Dr. Buchanan got to his feet but after a couple of steps staggered and slumped against the porch railing, clutching his face in his hands.

Paige jumped up from the sofa and rushed over to him. "Are you all right?" she asked.

"I'm fine. I'm fine," Nathan whispered, shielding his face from her view. Several minutes passed before he gradually straightened his shoulders and turned to Paige with a weak smile. "I'm sorry to have frightened you," he said. "It was clumsy of me but I almost lost my footing."

Confused, Paige stepped back from him just as Magda reappeared at the door. "I'm sorry to interrupt Nathan, but Kyle is waiting to speak with you." Slowly her eyes searched his face and fear gripped her features. "Did it happen again?" she asked, her speech almost inaudible.

"Yes," he answered softly, "but I'm all right now." With long, sturdy strides Nathan followed Magda into the house, leaving Paige on the porch with a distinct feeling something was terribly wrong.

Like the squirrel she had watched a few moments before, Paige listened intently to the wind whispering through the trees as if it carried an explanation of what had happened to Nathan Buchanan just a few minutes earlier. Had he merely slipped and lost his balance or had something more serious happened? She studied the tranquil view and zealously worked to calm her jagged nerves. Surely she had allowed her imagination to get the better of her.

After what seemed like an eternity, Dr. Buchanan returned to the porch carrying two fresh tall glasses of iced tea. "Now, that didn't take long, did it?" he asked, handing Paige a glass and sliding into the rocker across from her. He looked as happy and vibrant as ever. "No, it didn't take long at all," she answered, realizing he had been gone no longer than several minutes.

For a long time they sat quietly sipping their drinks and taking in the beauty of the countryside. Finally and reluctantly Dr. Buchanan broke the silence. "I've begun work on a book I'd like to complete by the end of the year," he said. "I call it the Rindleton Project. It requires an awful lot of research and documentation which is one of the reasons I've asked you to come to Austin early, Paige. Hopefully, between the two of us, we can get the majority of the legwork done by the end of summer. I'd like to get started as soon as possible. Are you ready to begin work?"

"Of course, Nat. Will you want me to teach classes at the college, also?"

"No, that won't be necessary. Summer teaching positions have already been filled. You'll begin your duties at the college in the fall." He was thoughtful for a moment. "What living arrangements have you made?" he asked.

"I'd planned to remain in the hotel until my furniture and car arrive from New York. Afterward, I'll find an apartment to rent."

"I see." Dr. Buchanan looked beyond her toward the hills in the distance. He knew he didn't have much time. He had to think of a way to speed up the completion of his book. "I'd planned to do most of the work on the project here at my home," he said, "and now suspect if we're to finish it on time, we'll have to toil very long hours. Would you consider moving in here for the summer, Paige? It would make things most convenient for both of us. Then, in the fall, when it's time for you to begin teaching your classes at Huston-Tillotson, you can find yourself accommodations in the city."

The prospect of spending the summer in the very same house the historian had grown up in appealed to Paige. "I'd like that," she said.

Dr. Buchanan smiled and winked at her. "Good. I'll have Magda prepare for your stay."

The next day Paige moved into the north second-floor bedroom of the Buchanan house. The room was spacious and charmingly furnished. A soft blue-and-white color scheme gave it a cool, refreshing air. The double bed was covered with a blue-and-white-checked spread and dust ruffle. Several pillows in various sizes and shapes rested at the head of the bed. In front of a small fireplace was a tea table and chair, and a mahogany secretary stood against one wall. Over-stuffed chairs were arranged on either side of the bed. Potted trees and oil paintings of happy clowns added to the attractiveness of the room. A deck, accessible through a set of french doors, looked out over the beautiful landscape.

Later that day Paige and Dr. Buchanan had lunch again in the cozy corner of the porch. And after a walk around the pond, they went into the library to begin work on the Rindleton Project.

Paige liked her new work area immediately. Although a wall had been removed and replaced with sliding glass doors, the room still possessed the warm elegance of the past. One wall held floor-to-ceiling bookcases filled to capacity with books, and the remaining walls were painted a rosy beige and accented with pastel paintings of the Texas countryside. Deep green sofas and rust-colored overstuffed chairs were arranged in conversational groupings along with heavy dark antique chests and tables. Dr. Buchanan walked over to his desk, which was piled high with papers, books and maps. Two tables stood adjacent to it and had obviously caught the overflow of materials. "This is the Rindleton Project," he smiled.

Paige lightly touched several stacks of papers with her fingertips. "I can't believe I'm actually about to begin work on one of your books."

"That's exactly what you're about to do," Dr. Buchanan told her. Leafing through some of the papers, he began to explain his new tome. "In this volume, we'll concentrate on the small town of Rindleton, which was founded in 1873 by former slaves," he said. "They established a gristmill and a general store in the middle of a farming community and prospered quite rapidly. Within a short period of time they built a church and a one-room schoolhouse which are standing today."

"The town is still in existence?"

"Oh, yes. We're going to trace Rindleton's history from its inception to the present point in time. In a few weeks I'll take you there for a tour and a chat with some of the descendants of the original settlers."

"Researching this project is going to be a heart-stirring experience," Paige said.

"I agree," Dr. Buchanan replied.

CHAPTER 3

Paige stepped into a pair of sand-colored high-heeled sandals and slipped on a classic white silk shirt and a softly gathered beige linen skirt. She brushed her hair, giving it a soft luster, and lightly made up her face. After inserting chunky gold earrings into her ears and dabbing a bit of Norell perfume at her throat and wrists she opened the french doors of her bedroom and stepped onto the deck.

The morning was clear and sunny and a fresh breeze stirred lazily. Viewing the Buchanan domain from her small private balcony after dressing for the day had become a ritual Paige enjoyed almost as much as she enjoyed working on the Rindleton Project. As she slowly savored the sweet fragrances of the colorful summer flowers and took in the beauty of the landscape, she glimpsed a large dark figure darting through a wooded area near the pond. Thinking she had sighted a deer or some other wondrous animal, Paige rushed back into her room and grabbed the binoculars from the secretary. Returning to the deck as quickly as she could manage, she aimed the glasses in the direction of the moving figure. For a second it was lost behind a clump of stubby trees before briefly reappearing and then dropping out of view once again. Disappointed she had been unable to see the animal well enough to identify it, Paige allowed the glasses to hang loose around her neck and directed her attention toward the hills in the distance. The natural beauty of the country-side was exhilarating, and she silently thanked Dr. Buchanan for giving her the opportunity to spend the summer in such splendid surroundings.

Shortly, the figure moved back into view and Paige quickly lifted the binoculars to her eyes and focused them. Instantaneously, she burst into soft giggles. Her great sighting was a man clad in navy-and-white jogging shorts running at an easy pace around the pond. She let the glasses slide from her eyes, a little disenchanted she hadn't seen some wild animal darting about in the woods. Nevertheless, her interest concerning the identity of the runner was aroused, and she again lifted the binoculars to her eyes and peered through them. From moment to moment the man moved nimbly among the trees making it difficult for Paige to discern any distinguishing features.

Finally, she left the deck and went quietly downstairs. Finding no signs of Dr. Buchanan or Miss Winslow, Paige ate a quick breakfast of fresh melon, toast and tea. She then made her way to the library and began work on the Rindleton Project. Paige decided to look into the educational system that existed in the town in the early 1920s and walked over to one of the side tables where she had sorted through materials and placed them in neat piles the day before. As she reached for a stack of papers, her attention was drawn to the outside of the sliding glass doors. The man whom she had seen jogging around the pond earlier that morning was now standing just a few yards away in the shade of the spreading oak tree.

With his hands resting casually on his hips he drew in several deep breaths, expelled them forcefully and then began stretching exercises. His skin, the color of ground cloves, glistened with perspiration as he worked diligently with the muscles in his long, well-developed legs. Instead of picking up the stack of papers that she had decided to study, Paige reached for the binoculars. Realizing what she was about to do, she pulled her hand away from them as if she'd been burned. Regardless, she continued to watch the man and eventually was drawn once again to pick up the glasses.

She trained them on his head which was covered with short, coarse raven-black hair. And his features came into her full range of vision when he grimaced and turned slightly. The man was gorgeous. Paige studied his strong, angular face and guessed he was about thirty-five years old. His eyes appeared to be large pitch-black pools, his nose which was somewhat crooked, flared softly at the nostrils, his lips were full and sensuous and his teeth were even and pearly white. Paige eased the glasses down a couple of inches bringing into view a strong neck, broad shoulders, a powerful, smooth chest and well-developed arms. His stomach was taut and flat and his hips were trim. She prepared to drop her gaze even farther but was interrupted.

"Good morning, Early Bird," Dr. Buchanan said, striding into the library. "How long have you been working?"

Embarrassed and surprised by his sudden appearance, Paige slammed the binoculars down on the table with such force she was sure she had broken them. "Good morning, well I . . . uh . . . I've been working for about twenty minutes. How are you, Nat?" she asked, with a nervous smile. She hoped he hadn't seen her studying the man under the oak tree through the binoculars. That would cause her a lot of embarrassment. Frankly, she couldn't imagine what had possessed her to act in such an irrational way, but she felt certain it would never happen again.

"Oh, I'm fine, Paige," Nathan Buchanan answered. "But I want to make certain you're not driving yourself too hard. We've worked long hours almost every day this week and it's about time you slowed down a little."

"Don't worry about me, Nat." Paige assured him. "I'm refreshed and ready to go."

"Good." He walked over and stood next to her. "Have you been checking on some of my little friends?" he asked, picking up the field glasses and gazing through them.

Dr. Buchanan *had* seen her watching something through the binoculars, but he had erroneously assumed it was some of the animals. She attempted to hide her discomfort as she forced herself to glance in the direction of the oak tree. The man was gone. "Yes, yes I was," she said, with a sense of relief. "I was watching a red bird."

"A red bird?" He seemed surprised and immediately Paige wondered if she had been caught in her lie. Surely there were red birds in the Texas hill country.

"Yes . . . well, I think it was . . . a red bird."

"Lucky you," he said, turning to look at her. "Did you make a wish?"

"Yes, I did," she replied, thoughtfully. She hated lying but was too embarrassed to tell the truth.

"Good girl. You do know that any wish you make on a red bird will come true," he told her, with a smile and a wink.

"I know," she laughed. She picked up a stack of papers and shuffled through them. "I'm going to do some more reading this morning," she said, "and later today I'll type your notes on Lucas Rindleton."

"That's fine. But I'm afraid you'll have to work alone for a while. Magda and I are driving into Austin and won't be back until late evening." He took both her hands in his. "Promise me you won't work too hard while I'm away," he said.

"I promise."

"All right. Your lunch is in the refrigerator. Don't forget to take time out to eat."

"I'll break for lunch."

He started out of the room and then hesitated. "I almost forgot to tell you, Paige, my nephew, Kyle, is here from Houston. He came in late last night and will be with us for a week or more. I wanted to introduce you two, but I think he's out jogging or something. At any rate, I've told him about you and I'm sure he'll come by to say hello. Maybe you can have lunch together."

"That would be nice." Paige smiled. She returned his wave as he left the room and then sank into the chair behind his desk with a sigh. Perhaps she had been working too hard, she thought, thumbing through the papers. What other explanation was there for her unusual behavior? It just wasn't like her to indulge herself by watching some man exercise. Each time she thought of the acute embarrassment it would have caused had someone seen her, she shivered. She was lucky no one had, especially Nat. Paige shifted positions in her chair and allowed herself to smile for a moment. So the handsome jogger had been Kyle Buchanan. What was he like? she wondered. She shook her head to clear her thoughts. She had to get back to work. Paige began reading her notes and before long was completely absorbed in the early educational system in Rindleton, Texas.

Three hours had passed when she finally put her materials aside and glanced at her watch. Deciding to take her lunch break, Paige got to her feet and started out of the library. But before she reached the door, Kyle Buchanan, dressed in a white cotton knit shirt and navy blue slacks, walked into the room. He looked like a black panther out for an afternoon stroll, his movements slow, sure and graceful. Paige froze and watched him move deliberately toward her, feeling as though she were prey being stalked for an evening meal. He stopped, directly in her path, so close, in fact, she could feel the heat of his body on hers and smell the fresh pine scent of his cologne. He peered unblinkingly into her face, and like a trapped animal she met his gaze. Her heart pounded rapidly and beads of perspiration covered her upper lip as she vainly attempted to tear her eyes from his.

"Round smoky-quartz disks with velvety-brown centers, suspended in white satiny pools and fringed with silky chocolate-colored threads. You have the most beautiful eyes I've ever seen." His voice was low and powerful and his breath fanned her face as he spoke.

Paige felt suddenly weak and her words faltered as she tried to speak. "I'm . . . I'm . . . Paige Avalon," she said.

"I know, Uncle's new teacher, research assistant and" —he moved away from her over to the table, picked up the binoculars, raised a brow and glanced out of the window—"bird watcher, or should I say weather girl?" Slowly he walked back to where she stood and looked straight into her large brown eyes. "Perhaps the most precise description of you would be man watcher." A smile played about the corners of his lips as he fastened his eyes on her. "Don't you know these things will magnify the object they're trained on twenty-five times?" he asked, waving the glasses around in the air. "Just what part of my anatomy were you studying anyway? Certainly you don't plan to include your findings in Uncle's project."

Her face burned with embarrassment. "I'm afraid I don't know what you're talking about . . . uh . . . what did you say your name is?" she asked, stalling for time. Her mind had gone blank and she couldn't think of how to defend herself.

"The name is Kyle Buchanan, and you do know what I'm talking about. I'm the guy you studied with these things when I was right outside the window there a few feet away. As a matter of fact we were so close we could have touched if that plate of glass hadn't separated us."

"You're flattering yourself, Mr. Buchanan," Paige said, gathering her wits about her. "The only thing I looked at through the binoculars this morning was a red bird."

"Come, come, Miss Avalon, a few hours ago you studied one part of my body or the other until your heart was content, or should I say up to the time my uncle came into the room."

Recognizing she would never convince him of the contrary, Paige spoke with cool indignation. "It appears that you were watching me when you were supposed to be exercising."

"I was exercising, but it was quite an eerie feeling having a beautiful woman watching every move I made through these things just a few feet away." He put the binoculars back on the table and stared at her.

"Once and for all I wasn't watching you exercise,"

Paige said, making one last attempt at persuading him he had been wrong about her. He was so overbearingly assuming she couldn't allow him to believe she had found him worth contemplating. "I only glimpsed someone, and now I know it must have been you, under the oak tree as I observed a bird on one of its branches. I'm sorry you feel that your body is so perfect and beautiful that I, or anyone else, would waste time watching you flex your muscles." Paige moved back to her desk. "Now if you'll excuse me I have to get to—"

"Thank you for the kind compliment," Kyle said, not allowing her to finish her sentence. "I work very hard to stay in shape." With a smile of victory tugging at his lips, he again moved within inches of her. "But I can't excuse you just yet," he continued softly. "Let's move on to more important matters. Is the name *Miss* Paige Avalon?"

"Yes," she answered, the tension between them growing the closer he moved to her. "Miss and Doctor," she added and then felt foolish after having said it.

Kyle's eyes swept over her curiously. "That title, Dr., means a lot to you, doesn't it?" His words were tinged with sarcasm.

"Yes it does," Paige retorted. She didn't care if he was Nathan Buchanan's nephew, his attitude was beginning to irritate her. "I've worked very hard for the title, and I'm proud of it."

"Hey, don't get excited, Dr. Paige Avalon," he said, raising both his hands as if defending himself from an attacker. "As a matter of fact, since you do have a title other than Miss, I'm relieved it's Dr. and not Mrs." He inched even closer.

His statement and nearness were causing Paige some discomfort. What game was he playing? Did he think he could do anything he wanted or say whatever he pleased to her just because she had watched him exercise earlier? She wished she had known then that he could easily see in the library from where he stood; she would have ignored him completely. "Why are you getting so close to me?" she demanded.

Kyle studied her for a moment. "Would you prefer that I step back a couple of feet and use the binoculars to zero in on my favorite spot the same as you did with me, this morning?" he asked coolly.

"Can't you forget this morning?"

A broad smile lit up his face. "If you'll agree to have lunch with me, I can forget whatever you'd like me to forget."

His challenge was appealing. She wanted to obliterate the morning episode conclusively. "Miss Winslow left some lunch in the refrigerator," she said, "would that interest you?"

"Yes, particularly since she prepared one of my favorite dishes."

"Then it's a deal," Paige said, extending her hand for him to shake.

Kyle clasped her fingers in his large hands, took them to his lips and kissed the tips lightly. "Good, I'll meet you on the porch in thirty minutes."

He left the library with long graceful strides. So that's what Nat's nephew is like, Paige thought, staring after him. Handsome and very sure of himself. Well, she couldn't waste time thinking about him. She had come to Austin to establish her career, and that was exactly what she was going to do. She would share lunch with Kyle Buchanan today so that she could forget the unfortunate morning incident, and after that she'd have to watch her behavior and keep it strictly professional.

Paige went to her room to freshen up before lunch. She brushed her hair, dabbed powder on her nose and brushed lip gloss on her lips. For several minutes she studied her face carefully. Although Paige had not worn eye makeup earlier, she now accented them with a bit of brown and pearl-white shadow. Feeling a little embarrassed she would go to such lengths to impress a stranger, she left her room for lunch.

She stepped out onto the porch and saw Kyle standing in a far corner leaning against the railing. Assuming an air of nonchalance Paige slipped her hands into her pockets and walked over to him. "Hi," she said. He seemed a little surprised when he turned and saw her.

"Hi, I thought you had decided to stand me up." His eyes swept her appreciatively.

"Not a chance," she told him, emphasizing every word.

His laugh was deep and musical. "That's right, we're quite serious about forgetting you know what." She gave him an icy stare. "Ooh, I love those eyes even when they're reflecting your anger," he said.

"I think we should get started with lunch," Paige told him, her tone crisp. "I have to get back to work."

"Of course." He walked her over to the table in the corner of the porch. "Why are you so dressed up?" he asked. "You should have on something cool like a sundress or shorts."

Paige looked shocked. "I'm not on holiday," she said. "I'm dressed for work. I'm a college teacher, a professional."

"I see." He held a chair for her while she slipped into it and then filled their glasses with lemonade from a pitcher sitting on the table.

"Miss Winslow makes wonderful drinks for warm summer afternoons," she said, sipping from her glass.

"Sorry to disappoint you, but I made the drink," Kyle informed her. "I was hoping you wouldn't find it too provincial."

"What an odd thing to say." She fixed him with a steady gaze. "Why should I think such a thing?"

He shrugged. "You're a teacher, a doctor, a professional. I thought a no-nonsense woman like you might require a different kind of drink with her lunch. Something more sophisticated, like champagne or whiskey."

Paige glared at him. "I like fruit drinks like this," she said, and took another gulp of the lemonade. "They're great thirst-quenchers."

"Good. I'm glad it meets with your approval." He shifted in his chair. "You know, for some reason your name seems very familiar to me."

"Perhaps it reminds you of those things you turn when you're reading a book or the paper. Or do you do anything as civilized as that?"

Kyle laughed. "I'm afraid I do an awful lot of reading," he said. "Nevertheless, I was referring to your surname not your first name."

"Oh, I see. Well, maybe Avalon seems familiar to you because you're still reading about King Arthur and the Knights of the Round Table."

"That's it," Kyle said, snapping his fingers. "The island of Avalon, the earthly paradise, where at death, King Arthur and other heroes were supposedly carried. Have you ever been there?" he asked.

"I don't believe you," Paige snapped, and got to her feet. "Let's eat!"

"I'll get lunch," Kyle laughed, encouraging her back into her chair.

"Oh, let me. After all it was my suggestion."

"It's no problem," Kyle told her. "I've already arranged everything." He went into the house and within minutes had returned with avocados stuffed with shrimp salad. Crisp, thin crackers encircled them.

"That looks good," Paige said, "but I feel guilty for not having helped you."

"It was no big deal, really. Miss Winslow had everything ready. All I had to do was fill the avocados with salad, take the crackers out of the box, put it all on plates and bring it out here. But if you're going to feel guilty about me serving lunch today, you can have the honors next time."

A curious frown knitted her brow. "What do you mean?"

"I mean we can plan to have lunch together again, since it looks like I'll be in Austin for a while."

"Business?" Paige asked, and then wanted to bite her tongue. She was showing entirely too much interest in Kyle Buchanan.

"Yes. Austin is the capital of Texas, you know, and the governor has called a special session of the state legislature. I may be here for a week or two. I usually live with Uncle when we're in session. He'd be insulted if I came to Austin and took a room in a hotel."

"I didn't know you were a . . . uh . . ."

"State representative," Kyle said, supplying the information Paige was groping for.

"Oh, I think that's wonderful."

Kyle raised his brows in surprise. "Have I finally impressed you?" he asked.

"Maybe."

"Well, in that case I'm a lawyer, too," he added quickly. "Do I get any points for that?"

For a moment Paige was thoughtful. "A half," she said finally.

"I guess that's better than nothing."

"I suppose it is."

To her surprise, they chatted amiably during their lunch and Paige found herself thoroughly enjoying Kyle's company. She was drawn to his warmth and sensitivity as well as his intelligence and vitality, but she had some difficulty coping with his penchant for teasing.

The two blue jays that usually dropped by the Buchanan porch each afternoon at mealtime made their customary appearance on the lawn just beyond their table. And Paige and Kyle fed them shrimp and crackers, which they devoured eagerly.

"Are you going directly back to work?" Kyle asked, beginning to clear the table.

"No. Nat and I usually take a walk following lunch. I think I'll walk today, also."

"Good. Wait for me and I'll join you. This will only take a second." Kyle went inside the house and Paige made her way down the porch steps and to the shade of the spreading oak tree where she had first seen him doing his cooling-down exercises. She dared to turn her gaze in the direction of the glass wall of the library. Again embarrassment slowly crept through her as she realized he had easily seen her watching him. "You kinda like this spot don't you?" he asked, taking her off guard.

"And you kinda like sneaking up on people," Paige retaliated, walking away from him toward the pond. She knew he was merely teasing, but couldn't help feeling put down.

"Hey, you're going the wrong way," Kyle called.

Paige turned and glared at him. "I always take this path."

"That's the very reason it's the wrong one for today. If you've been walking with Uncle, you've no doubt walked to the pond on every occasion. That's his favorite place, but there are some other lovely spots around here."

Reluctantly Paige went back to join him. "I don't have long," she said. "I have quite a bit of work to finish."

"Oh, take the rest of the day off, Uncle won't mind." Paige stopped in her tracks. "I would never do anything as irresponsible as that."

For a second their eyes locked. "Forgive me," Kyle said, an amused expression settling on his features. "It was a dumb suggestion to make to a lady who's a doctor, a teacher and a professional."

"Don't you ever quit?"

"Sure. I'll quit when you relax and stop defending yourself for being human." Paige tore her gaze from his. "Let's go," he said. She followed him through a stand of pine trees to a path shaded with overlapping branches of grand old oaks. A warm, frisky breeze cooled them as they played dodge with the scattered rays of sun that managed to peek through the thick green canopy. For a long time they walked in silence, moving deeper and deeper into the woods. "Truce?" Kyle asked finally. Paige nodded slowly and returned his smile. "Good." He seemed to sigh with relief.

"I'm sorry for being an old grouch," she said, with a shy glance, "but I just don't want to give Nat reason to think he's made a mistake in hiring me. I like my job here and would like to stick around for a while."

Kyle stopped and drew her to him. "Relax, Paige. My

uncle is a very kind and understanding man. Besides, he's told me he's pleased with your work. By the time you complete this project he'll probably give you a promotion and a raise." He laughed and kissed her lightly on the nose. "Now, let's enjoy our walk. I promise to get you back early."

"Good evening, Dr. Avalon, Mr. Kyle." Jessie Lowery, the caretaker, momentarily startled them.

"Hello, Jessie," Kyle said, eyeing the man closely. "How did you manage to sneak up on us?"

Although Jessie Lowery was only in his early fifties, deep lines etched his face and his thin shoulders were slightly bent by years of work as a laborer. "Oh, I wasn't on the trail, sir," he said, smiling at Kyle and shoving his hands into the pockets of his overalls. "I was there, at the edge of the woods and heard your voice. I thought I'd give you these." He held out his hand and three gold twenty-dollar pieces were in it.

"Jessie, this is fantastic," Kyle said, taking the coins. "Where did I lose them?"

"Down by the dock. I'm sorry I didn't find them all."

"Don't worry. You found these and we'll find the others. Thanks, Jessie."

"Sure, Mr. Kyle." The caretaker made his way back into the woods.

"That's quite a little treasure," Paige said, watching Kyle clean the dirt from the coins with his fingers. "Do you collect gold pieces?"

"No. A friend gave me five of these for my birthday, and as you can see I promptly managed to lose them."

"Oh, you'll find the others, too," Paige told him.

Kyle smiled. "Thanks for the reassurance," he said.

After traversing a series of hills and valleys they reached the top of a verdant knoll peppered with pink, yellow and white wild flowers. Paige gasped. "I had no idea this was back here," she said. They stood overlooking a clear blue lake that snaked its way through the rolling countryside.

"Come with me." Kyle guided her to a swing, made with heavy rope and a plank, that hung from the limb of a giant pecan tree.

"This is wonderful!"

"I thought you might like this place. I spend a lot of time here when I visit."

"Is this your creation?" She sat down on the weatherbeaten board and Kyle eased in beside her.

"Yes it is," he answered, setting them in motion and causing her to squeal like a child. With one hand Paige held tight to the rope and with the other she clung fast to Kyle's waist. "I should have thought of this sooner." He smiled.

His long, strong legs propelled the swing high into the air, affording them a sweeping view of the countryside. The happiness that filled Paige pushed out of her being all of her previous feelings of anxiety. Relaxed, she delighted in the to-and-fro movement of the swing.

At last Kyle brought them to a stop. "I haven't done that in years," she admitted breathlessly. "I'd almost forgotten what fun swinging can be." She turned to look at him and his large dark eyes held her gaze. Although her brain's command was to turn away Paige sat still and awaited his kiss as he moved purposefully toward her. Slowly, Kyle took Paige in his arms and held her close before covering her slightly parted lips with his own. His warm, tender kiss made her his captive, briefly. When he released her, she leaned against him with a soft sigh.

"You're as wonderful to hold as you are to look at," he

whispered. For a second, Paige clung to Kyle's taut torso, feeling all the while she had made a mistake in encouraging his kiss.

"We'd better get back," she said, getting to her feet.

"Must we?"

"Yes, Kyle. I really do have a considerable amount of work to complete today."

He pulled himself out of the swing. "All right. I'll take you back, but only because you insist. I'd much rather we spend the afternoon together here on the lake." Lacing his fingers with hers, Kyle led the way to the path that would take them to the house.

Paige was attracted to Kyle. She couldn't deny that fact. But she wasn't willing to embrace a new romantic friendship just yet. The wounds she suffered as a result of her break with Steven were barely healed, and she couldn't risk falling in love again.

How very arrogant, she thought stifling a chuckle. A kiss and a silly compliment from a proud stranger was throwing her off course. Surely she wouldn't have to worry about becoming involved with Kyle Buchanan. He was only being kind to his uncle's employee.

They arrived at the house and Kyle walked her to the library. "Take some time off tonight, Paige, and have dinner with me," he said. "We can go to Austin. You could use a change of scenery."

"I can't, Kyle. I'm going to turn in early tonight so that I can be fresh for work at my usual time tomorrow morning."

"Paige, tomorrow is Saturday."

"I know. But I've decided to work every day of the week, this summer, so that Nat and I will be ahead of schedule on the Rindleton Project by the time classes begin in the fall."

"I don't believe this. Does Uncle know what your plans are? Does he know how hard you're working?"

"I haven't discussed my plans with him, yet," Paige said. "However, I'm sure he'll approve them. He is as anxious as I am to complete the project."

"You'll have to take some time out for recreation and relaxation or you'll go mad," Kyle argued.

"I can't take any time off from my work," Paige said softly, "and don't worry, I won't go mad either."

Kyle sighed in exasperation. "In that case, I guess I'll have to settle for sharing lunch with you again on the front porch. One day next week?" he asked.

"Yes. I'll be here."

He cupped her face in his hands and kissed her softly on the lips. "I'll see you then," he whispered.

Kyle left the library and Paige crossed the floor to the desk. Kyle Buchanan, she thought with a smile, what a charmer. Slipping a sheet of paper into the typewriter, she began typing Nathan Buchanan's notes on Lucas Rindleton.

CHAPTER 4

"It's highly improbable that I would lose one paper out of a stack of twenty," Dr. Buchanan told David Tucker, a little annoyed with the young man for interrupting his walk. "Did you submit your report along with the other members of your class?"

"No, Dr. Buchanan. I had some trouble getting it typed and you gave me permission to turn it in at the end of the day and I did. I took my report to your office and put it in your hands just as you were about to leave for home. Don't you remember?"

"I'm sorry, David, I don't."

"I have no reason not to tell the truth," David Tucker said, nervously shifting his weight from one foot to the other. "I turned my paper in on time."

Dr. Buchanan clasped his hands behind his back as he studied the young man standing before him. "I have no record of your report," he said. "I'm afraid you'll just have to make plans to take the course again in the fall."

Distress filled David's eyes. "Look, Dr. Buchanan, I have to graduate this summer," he said. "I can't afford to come back to school in the fall. Besides, I have a job waiting for me in Dallas. I promised I'd start work in September."

"I'm sorry, David. There's nothing I can do to help you."

"Please, look for my report one more time," David

pleaded. "It has to be there in your office somewhere. I don't have the money for another semester of school."

"All right," Dr. Buchanan said, nodding his head slowly, "I'll look for it once more."

"Thanks, Dr. Buchanan." David smiled hesitantly and then walked away.

"He seems to be a nice young man, Nathan," Magda said.

"He is. And a very bright one, too. But I don't remember receiving his report."

"Perhaps in your haste to get home that day, you mislaid it," Magda suggested.

"Perhaps I did," Nathan said. "I'll give us both the benefit of the doubt and look for his report again next week."

Protectively, Nathan took Magda's hand in his and they resumed their walk along Town Lake Avenue. His awareness of her soft warm fingers pressing against his flesh sent a rush of excitement through him, bringing to mind the first time he had seen her. The night they met aboard ship Nathan had thought Magda was one of the most beautiful women he had ever seen. Radiant in a simple pale green silk gown and silver slippers, she had mesmerized him as she moved across the floor to the table where he was seated. Her first "hello" sent his heart racing and from that moment on he had known he would spend as much of his holiday at sea with her as she would permit. As it turned out, and to Nathan's surprise and delight, Magda was equally attracted to him.

Nevertheless, when the cruise ended and the ship dropped anchor in Florida, Nathan had reached a difficult decision. Feeling eighteen years was too much of a disparity in their ages, he prepared to say goodbye to the only woman to capture his interest since his wife's death.

But Magda had other ideas. After several months of work and leisure time together, Nathan rejoiced in his failure to keep Magda out of his life. When they agreed Magda would move to Greens Cove, Nathan had decided to ask her to be his wife.

Suddenly, however, his life had become a nightmare and he knew it would be cruel to ask Magda to marry him under the present circumstances. His grip tightened on her fingers as he realized he would soon have to give up the woman he loved.

"You're awfully quiet, Nathan. What's wrong?"

He smiled and pinched her nose. "Everything," he answered. Dropping her hand he slipped his arm around her, pulling Magda closer to him.

"It's not as bad as all that. There're still a number of things Dr. Campbell would like to try. With time, all of this will be cleared up completely. I'm confident of that."

"I'm afraid you're wrong this time, Magda. There's nothing Dr. Campbell or anyone else can do for me now."

"Nathan, don't talk that way." She stopped and turned to face him. "You must have faith that you'll be cured."

"We can't pretend any longer, Magda. Dr. Campbell has never treated a case like mine before, and he's been practicing medicine for over thirty years."

"That doesn't mean you won't get well."

"There's no evidence that I will, either."

"You have to exhaust all of your options, Nathan. Don't forget Dr. Campbell plans to discuss your case with specialists in the field."

"Yes. Yes, I know."

"And if his specialists can't come up with a satisfactory solution to your problem, then you'll have to go to the medical center in Houston. You can get help there. I'm sure of it."

"I can't go to Houston without involving Kyle," he argued. "You know that's something I don't want to do just yet."

"Kyle would want to know that you're ill, Nathan. It's not fair for you to keep this from him."

"He's busy with his law practice and his work in the legislature," he sighed. "I can't distract him now."

"Your nephew should know," Magda insisted. "Promise you'll talk with him as soon as this special session of the legislature is over."

His gaze shifted to the river and for a moment rested on its smooth blue-green surface. "I'll consider it."

"Good." Though his reply was ambivalent Magda was relieved by it. She started to walk away, but Nathan stopped her.

"You must understand something very clearly, Magda," he said. "You're a young and beautiful woman who deserves to have a man in your life who can make you happy. Under no circumstances will I burden you with my problem."

She pressed her fingers to his lips. "No more of that nonsense," she whispered. "I love you, Nathan, and I know that soon you'll be well."

His gaze held hers for a long time. "I won't ruin your life, Magda. If Campbell doesn't find some way to cure me soon, I want you to promise you'll leave me and Greens Cove. With time I'll grow progressively worse, and I can't tolerate the idea of you seeing me become a hopeless invalid."

Shaking her head, tears spilled from her eyes and she took his face in her hands. "I'll never leave you, Nathan," she said. "Never."

Sobs formed in his throat but he refused to allow them to escape his lips. Nevertheless, Nathan longed to cry for the woman he loved, and he longed to cry for himself as he realized the happy life they had envisioned for themselves would never come to pass. Expecting to see her features clouded with anguish, he allowed his eyes to settle on her face and saw instead an expression of love and desire. With large tender hands that slowly caressed her neck and back, Nathan pressed Magda hard against him. Their lips met in a series of deep probing kisses and they were lost in a vortex of passion. At length, he released her. "We'd better get back," he whispered.

CHAPTER 5

Nathan Buchanan crossed the room and gazed out of the window before turning to Paige, his eyes filled with mischief. "I think we should take the rest of the afternoon off, young lady, and go to Austin. We can stop by the college, pick up the materials we need and then spend the remainder of the day sight-seeing. You haven't seen Austin or Huston-Tillotson as yet, have you?"

"No I haven't, and your idea sounds wonderful."

"Good. We'll finish up here, have lunch and then be on our way."

Paige had been in the lovely old Buchanan mansion now for two weeks and at times it was difficult for her to believe she was actually working and residing in the same house with Nathan Buchanan. Occasionally she pinched herself to make sure she wasn't spinning dreams in her Riverside Drive apartment in New York City. Each day her enthusiasm for her work and her admiration for the esteemed historian grew as they toiled together over the Rindleton Project. Gradually, Dr. Buchanan collaborated with Paige only two or three hours a day, leaving her to do the bulk of the work alone. But Paige didn't mind. She loved her new job.

Though Kyle was still living in his uncle's house, Paige seldom saw him. Nevertheless, she had thought of the handsome young lawyer frequently. She couldn't wipe from her mind the pleasant memories of their lunch on the porch or their surprisingly beautiful walk to the lake. She couldn't forget his warm and tender mouth on hers or how his lips had felt against her skin when he brushed her fingertips with a kiss. The sight of his strong muscular body glistening with perspiration as he exercised under the spreading oak tree, the feel of him next to her while they sailed over the countryside in the swing and the sweet, heady perfume of him still haunted Paige. But she fought her desire to seek him out for a talk or a leisurely walk through the woods and instead concentrated on her research.

Paige and Dr. Buchanan completed their morning's work, had lunch on the porch and started across the lawn to the garage. But before they reached the car, Dr. Buchanan, with a sudden sweep of his arms slapped his hands over his face and staggered forward. Paige stared after him for a moment, stunned. At last, subduing a wave of fear that nearly paralyzed her, she walked calmly over to him and placed her hand on his arm. "What is it, Nat?" she asked softly.

Several minutes elapsed before Nathan Buchanan allowed his fingers to slip slowly down his face and come to a rest at his sides. Pale and apparently unnerved, he shook his head wearily. "It's nothing to worry about," he said, but his words were not convincing. Paige encouraged him to return to the porch where for a long time he sat with his head resting in his hands. "Forgive me," he said, finally raising his head and turning to look at her.

"There's nothing to forgive," Paige replied anxiously. She took his hand in hers in an attempt to comfort him, feeling all the while there was something desperately wrong with the elegant old professor. Paige wondered if he would ever trust her enough to tell her his problems. She wondered if and how she could help him. They sat hand in hand on the white wicker sofa staring into the distance but seeing nothing. Neither one of them heard Kyle walk out on the porch. Neither one saw his eyes fasten onto their entwined fingers.

"Am I interrupting something?" he asked, his tone forbidding.

"No, no, my boy, come join us," Dr. Buchanan said, waving Kyle over to where they sat. "What are you doing home this time of day?" The old gentleman's eyes brightened and the tension that had gripped his features released them as he watched his nephew move down the porch to a chair directly in front of him.

"I thought I'd see if Dr. Avalon was interested in keeping a promise she made last week. But I can see she's very busy doing her special kind of research right now."

Dr. Buchanan looked confused. "What are you talking about?" he asked. He released Paige's hand and began massaging his brows with his fingertips.

"Nothing that concerns you, Uncle. It's just a little joke between Dr. Avalon and me."

Kyle shifted his gaze to Paige and smiled, but she could see he wasn't amused. What she couldn't discern was the reason for his obvious displeasure with her. "If you assumed we could have lunch together today," Paige said, watching his expression closely, "I'm afraid I'll have to disappoint you. Nat and I ate half an hour ago."

"I see. Perhaps next time," he replied, fixing her with a stony gaze. "So, are you all through with work for the day?"

"Yes," Dr. Buchanan answered. "Paige and I are going to take the afternoon off to visit Huston-Tillotson and explore Austin."

"Sounds like a fun afternoon. Enjoy yourselves."

"Thank you, we will." Nathan Buchanan got to his feet. "Shall we go, Paige?"

"Are . . . are you sure we should?" she asked, apprehension clouding her large brown eyes.

"Of course. Everything's fine, now. Come," he smiled.

She followed him to the steps and then hesitated, "If you have time tomorrow, Kyle," she said, "I'm sure I can arrange things so that I can honor my promise then." He smiled but said nothing.

Taking the same path they had taken earlier, Paige and Dr. Buchanan crossed the yard to the garage and climbed into the long black Lincoln. As they rode along Paige searched her mind for the reasons Kyle was acting so strangely. Had she said or done something to offend him? If so, what? And when? What did he mean by her special kind of research? Unable to come up with satisfactory answers, Paige turned her attention to the scenery. She was completely engrossed in the ranches, hills and the clear blue lake in the distance when suddenly she heard Dr. Buchanan moan, "Oh, no, not again. Not now." Just then the Lincoln swerved, crashed against something and rolled over several times before coming to a stop in a ravine.

Paige came to with a deep throbbing at her temples and a terrible ache at the back of her head. She had been pulled out of the car and was lying on a grassy knoll. She struggled to get to her feet but found her arms firmly pinned to the ground by two ladies on either side of her. "What happened?" she asked, her voice barely a whisper. "Where's Dr. Buchanan? Is he all right?"

"Calm down," one of the ladies said. "You've had an accident, but neither you nor your companion appears to be seriously hurt."

"Thank God," Paige whispered with relief. She turned slightly and a sharp pain shot through her head causing her to grimace until the discomfort subsided. When she opened her eyes again she could see Dr. Buchanan sitting on the side of the road holding a white cloth to his forehead. It appeared to be stained with blood, and immediately Paige became excited. "You told me he was all right," she accused, "and he's bleeding. Let me go to him," she pleaded. "You've got to let me go to him."

"He's going to be okay," the older woman told her. "Now relax. We've called for help. Some one will be here soon."

With a feeling of complete helplessness, Paige began to sob, which caused her head to ache even more. Someone promptly placed a cold wet towel on her forehead and within a short period of time her weeping ceased. Though her head still ached, she slowly began to relax and look about her. Through the small crowd of people that had gathered at the scene she could see the shiny black sedan resting on its side just a few feet away. The right front end had been severely damaged. "Did we hit another car?" she asked. "Was anyone hurt?"

"No other car was involved," a kind voice told her. "For some reason you ran off the road and hit a tree."

Relieved, Paige remained in a lying position on the grass, unable to do anything else with the two ladies restraining her. She adjusted her gaze so that she could see Dr. Buchanan. The cloth that he was holding to his head was becoming more and more blood-stained as he folded and unfolded it several times and pressed it to his injury. A tall man with a deep suntan and thick straight black hair sat next to him talking softly. Unaware of the span of time that elapsed between her becoming aware of the ladies at her sides and the arrival of the police car and ambulance, Paige lay in a daze trying to determine what had happened. She recalled thinking about the blue-green lake they were driving toward and how nice it would be to take a swim in it just before she heard Nat groan, "Not again." She could remember nothing after that. What had happened to him? Had he succumbed to another one of his strange attacks? She struggled in vain to answer the questions that repeatedly popped into her head.

The ladies released Paige's arms, and paramedics quickly and skillfully examined her. At last she was allowed to sit up. "Feeling better?" one of them asked.

"Yes," Paige answered. They helped her to her feet, and on very shaky legs she made her way over to Dr. Buchanan.

"Were you hurt?" he asked, as she knelt at his side.

"Just a bump on the head." She managed a weak smile. "But I'm okay. How about you?" She longed to hear that he was all right.

"I'm about the same," he said. "Only my bump decided to bleed a bit." He removed the cloth, and with relief Paige could see he had sustained only a superficial wound.

The wrecker pulled the sedan out of the ditch, and after Nathan talked briefly with the policemen, he and Paige climbed into the truck and were taken back to the house.

Magda Winslow was sitting on the porch when the

tow truck pulled into the driveway. She rushed to the steps and waited as Paige and Dr. Buchanan crossed the lawn to where she stood. "What happened?" she asked. "Did you have another—?" Tears came to her eyes, and she didn't bother to finish her question. She clamped her hands over her mouth and led the way into the house. "Go into the library," she said. "I'll bring you something cool to drink."

Like small children, Paige and Dr. Buchanan obeyed Magda's orders. "It was very selfish of me to try to drive into Austin," he said, easing onto the sofa with a deep sigh, "but I had just had an attack and didn't expect another one so soon."

With trepidation Paige asked what she had wanted to ask for some time, "What kind of attack did you have, Nat?"

He stared at his hands that were laced together and resting between his knees. "I have essential blepharospasm, Paige."

Her mouth dropped open as she sat down beside him. "What?"

The shock and fear reflected in her voice caused Nathan Buchanan to shift his gaze to his young companion. As he studied her face he realized his words had terrified her. "Don't look so distressed," he said, "it's not contagious." He laughed and patted her hand.

"Please don't tease me, Nat," Paige said, her large eyes filling with tears.

"Of course. You've never heard of essential blepharospasm," he replied, his tone serious once again. "Most people haven't."

Miss Winslow brought them frosted glasses of cinnamon iced tea. "Nathan, love," she said, sitting next to him and caressing his brow, "I knew I should have

insisted on driving you to Austin today. I'll never forgive myself for what has happened."

"Now, now, Magda, it's not your fault," he chided
gently. "I've been feeling very well lately and I thought
I could make the trip safely."

"We both should have known better," she insisted.
"Please don't ever take another foolish chance like that
again."

Attempting to reassure her, Nathan kissed her lightly
on the cheek. "I'll be careful, Magda," he said. "I promise. Now, leave Paige and me alone for a while. I think I
owe her a long overdue explanation for my strange
behavior."

"Certainly. I'll be in the kitchen if you should need
me." They kissed briefly before Magda left the library.

Besides feeling like an eavesdropper on Magda Winslow and Nathan Buchanan, Paige was shocked by the
interchange between them. Never, during her short
stay at the lovely old mansion, had she suspected they
were anything more than employer and employee. She
stared after the attractive "handywoman" as she
moved across the room and out of the door. They make
a very handsome couple, she thought, warmed by the
realization of their love for each other.

Dr. Buchanan cleared his throat noisily and immediately regained Paige's attention. "I think we were discussing essential blepharospasm before Magda interrupted us," he said, sipping thirstily from his glass. "To
put it simply, Paige, it's a condition where the eyelids
unexpectedly and uncontrollably slam shut and can't
be opened again for several minutes."

"Oh, Nat, how awful."

"This problem is the reason why I've been pushing so
hard to complete the Rindleton Project as soon as possi-

ble. I'm not sure how long I'll be able to continue to
work."

"But what causes it? Can't your doctor help you?"

"He's trying to help me with medication, but as you
have observed, it's not working."

"There has to be something he can do."

Dr. Buchanan closed his eyes and rested his head
against the back of the sofa. "Well, we are trying another remedy. I've begun psychoanalysis. Pray that it's
effective, Paige."

The tears that had filled her eyes spilled onto her face
as she gazed at her mentor. Why did something as terrible as this have to debilitate such a brilliant and productive man? Surely there was something else that could
be done. She dried her eyes and drank thoughtfully
from the crystal glass. Did Kyle know his uncle's medication was ineffective? If so, why didn't he protest
when he saw him climb behind the wheel of the car? At
that moment Paige realized she was not the only one
Dr. Buchanan was attempting to hide his illness from.
Kyle was as oblivious of his uncle's dilemma as she had
been. But why? It was too dangerous an illness to be
kept secret. "Nat, you should explain all of this to Kyle,"
Paige said.

Nathan Buchanan sat up abruptly and grasped Paige
by the hands. "No. And you mustn't tell him. Promise
me, Paige, that you'll keep what you've learned here
today secret."

"But why? Shouldn't Kyle know you're ill?"

"No," he repeated emphatically. "My nephew is
working very hard right now, and I don't want him
distracted. He's sponsoring a bill in the House of Representatives and I want his mind free to concentrate on
his work. And when he returns to Houston I don't want

him worrying about me here in Austin." Pensive, he slumped against the sofa. "Magda knows and now you know. I refuse to burden anyone else with my problem. Please, Paige, what I've been forced to tell you is confidential."

"Yes, of course," she agreed unwillingly.

Kyle stood in the doorway of the library and stared at the couple on the sofa. His eyes fastened on their joined hands and moved rapidly upward to their faces as if he were desperately attempting to determine what was transpiring between them.

"Oh, Kyle," Magda said, walking up behind him, "would you like a cold drink?" He looked at her blankly. "Nathan and Paige are having iced tea," she went on. "Are you going to join them?"

"Yes, yes I think I will," he said, gazing at Magda as if he were seeing her for the first time in his life.

"I'll get you a glass."

"Thank you," Kyle replied absently. He entered the room and went to stand in front of Dr. Buchanan. "I seem to be making a habit of barging in on you, today, Uncle," he said, "but I was on my way out for the afternoon and got only as far as the garage. I saw the sedan. What happened?"

"There's nothing to fret about," Nathan answered, surprised to see his nephew. He continued hastily, "Paige and I started to Austin, and as I rounded a curve and climbed a hill I lost control of the car. You know I've driven that road thousands of times, Kyle. I guess it was just my time to have one of those freak accidents."

"Are you all right?" Kyle asked, concerned, his eyes moving from his uncle to Paige and then back to his uncle again.

"Paramedics came to the scene of the accident and
checked us out," Dr. Buchanan told him. "We're fine."
Magda brought Kyle a glass of iced tea and as he took
it from her he sat down in one of the chairs across from
the sofa. Momentarily, she studied his face and with a
quick glance at Dr. Buchanan silently left them. "Perhaps you should get a second opinion," Kyle said.

"That won't be a problem. Tomorrow, Magda will
drive me to see my doctor for my annual checkup. I'll
find out then if those youngsters missed anything."

"Good." Kyle directed his attention to Paige. "What
about you? Don't you need another examination, also?"
His voice reflected a mild hostility as he fixed his eyes
on her.

"I suppose you should get a second opinion, Paige,"
Dr. Buchanan said, confused by his nephew's tone.

"I can take her to see Dr. Foster, tomorrow," Kyle
offered.

His uncle looked pleased. "That's an excellent idea.
But will you have time?"

"Yes, and I'll be glad to help out."

"Great. And while you're in Austin maybe you can
stop by the college and pick up that box of materials we
were supposed to get today."

"We will, Uncle. Don't worry about anything."

Paige felt as though she were invisible because the
men made plans for her as if she wasn't sitting there.
But she didn't challenge them for fear of upsetting Dr.
Buchanan even more.

"Thank you, Kyle. Now, if you two will excuse me,
I'm going upstairs to rest."

Kyle got to his feet and walked his uncle to the door.
"I'll come by to see you when I get in tonight," he told
him.

"Sleep well, Nat," Paige said softly. The affection in her voice was not missed by the younger man or Magda Winslow who stood at the library door.

Kyle returned to his chair and fixed Paige with a cold penetrating gaze. "So, what is this between you and my uncle?" he asked, his voice low and angry.

Paige stared at him, her mouth ajar. She was beginning to have body aches from the car accident, and she was still mentally numb from what Dr. Buchanan had just told her about his illness. Suddenly she felt very tired. Why was Kyle so angry with her?

"What are you talking about?" she asked.

"Why did my uncle have that accident?"

"He told you. For some crazy reason he lost control of the car."

"I don't believe it. There was some other cause for that smashup and I intend to find out what it was." He leaned forward in his chair. "What were you trying to do to him while he was driving?" he questioned.

Her large round eyes stretched in amazement. "What on earth are you talking about, Kyle?"

"I'm talking about your motives, Dr. Avalon. Why did you move into my uncle's home? Why did he wreck his car on a road he's driven all his life?"

Paige closed her eyes and took several deep breaths. "What are you accusing me of?" she asked calmly.

"Nothing, yet. I'm merely asking questions. Are you beginning to feel guilty or don't you have a conscience?"

"I can't fathom what you're getting at, Kyle Buchanan. And I'd appreciate it if you'd be man enough to come out with what's on your mind."

"I think I've made myself clear, Paige. Neither of the questions was phrased to conceal its meaning."

"Then, none of it's your concern," she snapped angrily. Paige wasn't sure what she was being accused of, but she did realize the charges were uncomplimentary and she didn't like them.

"Oh, but the health and welfare of my uncle are very much my concern," Kyle retaliated.

"You're trying to make me defend myself for some insane figment of your imagination." Then with a feeling of exhaustion overtaking her, Paige decided to counter Kyle's rudeness with cool intelligence. "I moved into your uncle's house because he asked me to," she said. "He's been concerned about completing the Rindleton Project on time and thought that by my living here we could work together longer hours than would be possible if I lived in the city."

"That doesn't sound like Uncle. He's a competent man and has completed enough books and articles not to feel pressed about a deadline. Why has he chosen this particular one to overly concern himself with?" When Paige did not answer, he pressed on, "And he's had any number of research assistants. What makes you so special you have to move into the house with him? None have in the past."

"I don't know," Paige sighed, aching to tell him the truth.

"I think you do," Kyle said, getting up from his chair and crossing the floor to sit next to her on the sofa. "I think you've made plans to seduce and marry my uncle. You're an opportunist, Dr. Avalon, and see Nathan Buchanan as a means of securing a prestigious place for yourself in the academic arena. But I'll not have him hurt."

For a moment Paige felt faint, and she quickly took a

large swallow of iced tea. "What have I done to give you such a horrible idea?"

"You've persuaded Uncle to let you move in here so that you can be near him night and day. And although you pretend to be dedicated to your work, everytime I see you, you're holding his hand."

Slowly it began to dawn on Paige that twice that day Kyle had seen Dr. Buchanan and her holding hands. But it was hard for her to believe that he actually thought she was interested in seducing and marrying his uncle. She respected the historian too deeply to attempt something as devious as that. "Sometimes things are not what they seem," she said. "Nat is a very attractive man and yes I adore him, but under no circumstances could I ever do what you're suggesting. My esteem for your uncle would never allow me to deceive him in such a way. I'm not looking for a marriage of convenience, Mr. Buchanan," she said. "I'm perfectly capable and willing to work for my success." She rose from the sofa and walked toward the door. "I'm not romantically interested in Nathan Buchanan or any man right now and won't be for years to come. My love object is my work," she told him smoothly.

Paige was oblivious to the light of challenge that began a slow burn in Kyle Buchanan's searching dark eyes as he got to his feet and turned to meet her gaze. "We'll see, Dr. Avalon," he said. "We'll see."

"Now if you'll excuse me I'm going to my room to lie down."

"Ten o'clock tomorrow morning?" he asked coolly.

Paige felt confused. "Oh yes," she finally answered, remembering the plans made earlier. "Ten o'clock tomorrow will be fine."

CHAPTER 6

The sun had just risen above the trees when Kyle began a slow jog around the pond. He was tired and edgy after spending most of the night pacing the floor of his room mulling over the relationship between Paige and his uncle. Was he wrong about her? Was hard honest work her only objective for being at Greens Cove? Or did she have plans to exploit Nathan Buchanan and quickly establish herself on the academic stage?

Paige was a beautiful and intelligent young woman. Why would she want to devote her life to her work? Didn't she desire or need more? What about a husband? A family? It was all rather incredible, he thought. There had to be a young man in her life. Who was he? Where was he? Surely she wouldn't chance tying herself down with someone old enough to be her grandfather just to make a name for herself. More than anything Kyle wanted to believe Paige had told him the truth about her feelings for Dr. Buchanan.

Nevertheless, Paige's relationship with his uncle wasn't Kyle's only concern. For the first time since his uncle's accident, he allowed himself to wonder whether or not someone had tampered with the sedan. The longer and harder he thought about the idea the more troubled he became.

After his six-mile run and cooling-down exercises, Kyle made his way to Jessie Lowery's rooms above the garage. With the knuckle of his forefinger he tapped softly on the door. It swung open immediately and the caretaker, dressed in his customary overalls, white shirt and wide-brimmed straw hat stepped out on the porch.

"Good morning, Mr. Kyle," he said. "What are you doing up so early?"

Kyle sat on the edge of the porch and the caretaker followed suit. "I'm looking for answers, Jessie. Perhaps you can help."

"I'd be happy to do whatever I can."

With a worried glance Kyle asked, "Do you think anyone meddled with Uncle's car yesterday?"

"Absolutely not, Mr. Kyle," Jessie answered, taken aback by the question. "I ran a few errands in that car just before Dr. Buchanan and Dr. Avalon left Greens Cove and it drove perfectly all right."

"I see. You haven't noticed anything of a suspicious nature around here have you?"

"No, sir. Not a thing."

"Okay, Jessie," Kyle said, getting to his feet. "I just thought I'd check out all possibilities. Keep this conversation under your hat, will you? I don't want to concern Uncle unnecessarily. And if you should come across anything that may indicate he's in some kind of danger, please let me know pronto."

"Will do, Mr. Kyle." The caretaker followed him down the steps. "By the way," he said, "have you found your other gold coins, yet?"

"No, I haven't."

"Then, I'll continue to keep an eye out for them, too, sir."

"Thanks, Jessie."

Kyle returned to the house, showered and changed his clothes. For some reason he just couldn't accept Nathan's explanation of the accident. There had to be a sound reason for his running off the road he'd driven almost daily for so many years. Was someone trying to hurt him? Had Nathan failed a student who should have passed? Or give someone a grade who deserved another? Were any of his colleagues jealous of his accomplishments? He searched his thoughts but couldn't come up with a satisfactory answer. Nevertheless, the feeling that his uncle hadn't told the whole truth still nagged him. He had to find out why. And, if the Lincoln hadn't been tampered with, he finally decided, then he'd have to conclude that somehow Paige had been the cause of the accident.

With the light pressure of his fingers at her elbow, Kyle escorted Paige across the small parking lot to his red Ferrari. He helped her into the black leather bucket seat and quickly made his way round the car and under the wheel. "What did Doc Foster have to say?" he asked, a deep frown etching his brow.

Relieved the examination was over, Paige exhaled audibly. "I'm in perfect shape," she said.

"You paid him to tell you that? What a waste. I could have given you the very same information free of charge. What did he do? Make his diagnosis by just looking at you?"

A cool smile played at the corners of Paige's lips. "Dr. Foster checked me quite thoroughly and found no injuries as a result of the accident yesterday."

"That's good to know. I hope Uncle gets the same terrific news."

"Oh, I'm sure he will. After all, Nat didn't seem the least bit hurt yesterday other than the cut on his forehead." She watched Kyle start the engine of the sports car and guide it into the flow of traffic, hoping she had put his mind at ease concerning his uncle's health. Nevertheless, she, too, was deeply troubled about Dr. Buchanan. He had suffered a blow to his head which could possibly cause his eye condition to worsen. She dreaded the thought that the accident might induce more frequent attacks. She had no insight into the strange disease of essential blepharospasm. What caused it? Would Dr. Buchanan ever be cured? While they drove along the freeway Paige toyed with the idea of telling Kyle of his uncle's illness. It distressed her to think he could have an even more serious accident as a consequence of one of his attacks. If that happened, she would never forgive herself. But could she betray Dr. Buchanan's trust? The question threw her into a state of mental turmoil.

"Are you okay?" Kyle asked, giving Paige a cursory glance.

"Yes, of course. Why do you ask?"

"You seem distracted."

"Personal problem." Paige smiled. "Sorry."

"That's all right. May I be of some help?"

"No, but thanks for offering."

"Any time." Their eyes locked for a moment. "I think I'll take a stab at changing your cheerless mood and making those big beautiful brown eyes of yours light up," Kyle said.

"Oh?"

"To your left, Dr. Paige Avalon, is Huston-Tillotson College."

A slow smile creased Paige's face as she gaped at several red brick buildings nestled among beautifully landscaped rolling green hills. "I completely forgot we were supposed to stop by here today," she said.

Kyle drove onto the charming campus of the small

college and parked the car. "I knew this would get your full attention and lift your spirits," he told her. "Let's take a stroll before going to Uncle's office."

He linked his arm with hers and they followed a footpath up a gentle rise. On either side of the pavement was a blending of the old and the new. Some buildings dated back to the early nineteen hundreds and others only several years old. Huge shade trees peppered the quadrangle, and under some of them were students engaged in conversation or study. At the summit of the hill the view of the city was breathtaking, and after spending some time drinking in the beauty of the region Kyle and Paige started back down the walk.

"Kyle, what are you doing here?" A dark, stocky man in his late forties approached them.

"Hi, Thomas." The two men shook hands and Kyle introduced Thomas Cox to Paige, explaining that he was head of the music department at Huston-Tillotson and a very good friend of his uncle's.

"Well, well, you look so snazzy I thought you were a new student," Thomas said.

Paige grimaced. "I'll have to do something about that. The very last thing I want is to be mistaken for a student."

"Please, Paige, don't change a thing," Thomas told her. "You're a sight for sore eyes. It'll be a pleasure to have a beautiful and stylish addition to our faculty. And there are a couple of bachelors around here who I know will thank Nat personally for hiring you."

"Tell them not to waste their time with this lady," Kyle said hastily. "Paige isn't interested in involving herself with any man, just now."

"That may be so, but at least allow my young friends to enjoy the chase," Thomas smiled. He tore his eyes from Paige and focused on Kyle. "Are you in Austin for the special session of the legislature?" he asked.

"Oh yes, and things are getting pretty rough. Looks like we'll be here for a second week."

"I understand you're doing some exciting things, Kyle. We're all very proud of you."

"Thanks, Thomas." They said their goodbyes, and Kyle and Paige continued their walk.

"I take it you're an important and influential person in Texas politics," she said.

"Only with Uncle and his friends," Kyle laughed.

"I see." But from what Dr. Buchanan and Miss Winslow had told her about him, Paige was beginning to feel that Kyle was something of a political figure in Texas and wondered just how powerful he really was. She stepped off the pavement and went to stand in the shade of one of the stately old trees, her thoughts going back to the snide remark he had made about her to Thomas.

"You were rude to poke fun at me to your friend," she said, when Kyle came to stand beside her.

Stunned, he opened his mouth. "What are you talking about, Paige?"

"The 'tell them not to waste their time,' bit. What did you mean by it?"

"I don't speak in code," he answered, an edge to his voice. "I've told you that once. I said what I said because you've made yourself quite clear about your professional image and career."

She glared at him. "You should have reminded me this morning we were coming by the college today. I would have changed into something more appropriate. I suppose you've been laughing at me ever since I got in the car." She realized she had made a stupid remark, but her pride wouldn't allow her to retract it.

Resting his hands on his hips, Kyle threw his head back and breathed deeply. "You know, Dr. Avalon, it never occurred to me that you weren't properly dressed to come by here and pick up a box of Uncle's papers," he said, adjusting his gaze to meet hers. "I guess that's because of my own casual attire, which I'm sure you haven't noticed."

The understatement of the day, Paige thought. She had certainly noticed how attractive Kyle looked in his snug-fitting white slacks and shrimp-colored knit shirt. "I hate being mistaken for a student," she snapped.

"Maybe Thomas thought you were a student because you are rather young, Paige."

"And not properly dressed."

Kyle studied her carefully, for a moment. "Frankly, I think you look exceptionally attractive and professional in your little Bermuda shorts and long socks." She sneered at him and made her way back to the footpath. "And another thing," he said catching up with her, "you made a drastic mistake when you pulled your hair back and knotted it, this morning." They walked a few feet more before Kyle stopped and turned Paige to him. Slowly, he began to loosen her hair.

"Kyle, what are you doing? Stop it!"

He caught her hands and held them. "Since I've already been blamed for how you look today I might as well fix you the way I like you." Her hair tumbled to her shoulders and he fluffed it about her face with his fingers. "Mmm, you're lovely," he whispered, with a smile.

"For your information," she said, through tight lips,

"I pinned my hair up this morning because that's how I choose to wear it."

"I like it down." Their eyes met and locked.

"What's your point?" Paige asked, flustered.

"No point, just preference." He took her by the arm, "Come on, let's go."

Paige followed Kyle into an old ivy-covered building, adjusting the rolled-up sleeves of the white shirt she wore. Her thoughts were rapidly shifting from her inappropriate attire to Kyle's unpredictable behavior. Only yesterday he had bitterly accused her of the most vile thing she could imagine, scheming to seduce and marry Nathan Buchanan for professional advancement and security. Why did he think she was capable of such an abominable act? Yes, he had seen them holding hands on a couple of occasions, but had he ever stopped to consider that perhaps they were doing so in order to comfort each other for some platonic reason or because there was genuine mutual fondness between them? Why had he concluded she was expressing affection for his uncle for an ulterior motive? The idea angered and disgusted Paige. After all, Nathan Buchanan was a very attractive man. Couldn't Kyle see that any woman, young or old, could be inclined to want to marry the historian simply because she loved him? And what about Magda Winslow? Had he forgotten his uncle was in love with her?

Regardless, Paige hoped she had made it clear to Kyle that she was not romantically interested in Dr. Buchanan. Surely he understood that though she was determined to accomplish her professional goals she would never abuse her relationship with him.

But how was she to interpret his present behavior? Was his teasing meant to make her look and feel foolish or help her to laugh at herself? Perhaps, Paige reflected, at the present time, she was as suspicious of Kyle's motives as he was of hers.

They walked the length of a long hall and made their way through a set of wooden double doors. Standing at a desk in a far corner of the office was a tall, thin woman with a brown-ocher complexion and very short curly black hair.

"Kyle Buchanan," she drawled, "did you finally get lucky? What a good-looking couple you two make."

"I wish," Kyle laughed. "I'm afraid Lady Luck is still holding out on me. Ann Fletcher, meet your new compeer and Uncle's research assistant, Paige Avalon."

The woman reached across the desk and shook Paige's hand. "It's nice to meet you," she said, "and welcome to the fold. Will you be working with us this summer?"

"No," Paige answered. "Right now I'm working with Nat on one of his projects. But I'm looking forward to teaching classes in the fall."

"I'm sure you'll enjoy it here," Ann told her. "Nat is wonderful to work for, and the college seems to attract bright and highly motivated students."

"While you ladies gossip about Uncle and the history department," Kyle said, "I'll check his office for that box of materials he needs."

Paige liked the friendly, outgoing Ann Fletcher right away and felt quite comfortable talking with her about Huston-Tillotson, Dr. Buchanan, the students and living in Austin.

"Were you fortunate enough to find an apartment close by?" Ann asked.

"I haven't looked for a place, yet," Paige explained. "For the time being I'm living at Nat's home in Greens

Cove. But I'm expecting my furniture and car to arrive from New York any day now, and I'll need an apartment then."

"Housing is difficult to find in Austin," Ann said, "because this is a college town. As a matter of fact, there are several colleges here and the students usually make apartments pretty scarce. But I may be able to help you. How large a place are you looking for?"

"Three or four rooms will be big enough for me," Paige said, her brows furrowing with worry.

"Then I have a deal for you. My sister's company is transferring her to Virginia and she'll be moving out of her three-room apartment next week. She lives only fifteen minutes from here by freeway. Interested?"

"Are you kidding?" Paige asked. "Miss Winslow, Nat's uh . . . housekeeper, has told me about the housing problem here and I had become a bit worried about finding a place."

"I hope Susan's apartment will solve that problem for you. If you'd like, I can show it to you Tuesday."

"Oh, I'd love that, Ann."

"Good. Why don't you make plans to spend the evening in Austin. We can take a look at the apartment and then have dinner at my place." She wrote her address on a sheet of paper and gave it to Paige. "Six o'clock?" she asked.

"I'll be there," Paige answered.

Kyle came out of his uncle's office carrying a brown cardboard box of books, magazines and papers. "I made several telephone calls and read a couple of articles trying to give you time to discuss everything and everybody," he announced, resting the box on Ann's desk. "Did you finish?"

"Not yet," Ann replied coolly. "We still have to dissect the handsome and eligible Kyle Buchanan."

Kyle looked at Paige and inadvertently she met his gaze. Instantly she knew she wasn't going to like what he was about to say. "Don't waste your time, Ann," he said, "this lady isn't interested. She's a doctor, a teacher, a professional."

Paige tried to smile, but somewhere in the process her lips refused to cooperate and she smirked instead. "Don't look so disgusted, Paige," Ann said, laughing gaily. "We all know Kyle likes to tease. That's one of the techniques he uses in the legislature to wear down his opponents. He torments them until they give in. Sometimes he practices on innocent citizens, like you, but once you learn to handle him, he'll back off."

"Please, don't give her any ideas," Kyle said, picking up the box and walking to the door. "See you later, Mrs. Fletcher."

"Goodbye, you two. Enjoy your day."

Paige followed Kyle out of the building and to the car. "Are you angry with me?" he asked, once they settled themselves.

"Was that your objective?"

"No. I guess I'm just trying to find out what you're made of." He drove to Seventh Street and then the freeway.

"You're using the wrong approach."

"I've gathered as much. Will you give me a chance to redeem myself?"

Paige shot him a sidelong glance. "Sure. Go ahead. It'll be interesting to see what you're clever enough to come up with."

Kyle laughed softly. "I feel like I'm on trial." With a self-satisfied smile, Paige held his gaze. "All right," he said, clearing his throat, "let's start with lunch." He maneuvered the sports car off the freeway and drove a short distance to the Glass Dome, a restaurant that sat isolated in a deep valley and overlooked a clear blue lake.

They were seated at a lakeside table and quickly served the chilled dry white wine that Kyle ordered. "So far, so good," Paige said, looking about her at the clean modern lines of the elegant red-and-white room.

"Good. May I propose a toast?" Kyle asked, lifting his glass.

"I have absolutely no need for your phony salutations."

"All right," he breathed. "Shall I order for you?"

"Yes. I'd like that."

He studied the menu and gave his selections to the waiter while Paige gazed out of the window. In the thickly wooded area that surrounded the lake she could see deer darting friskily about. The view was so beautiful it seemed totally unreal.

"Now, the die is cast. Hopefully I haven't made any serious mistakes." He smiled at her. "What's a safe topic for discussion?"

"The ball is in your court."

"Mmm, I have a feeling the ball is going to stay in my court all evening. That's no way to play a tennis game, you know." Paige wrinkled her nose and waited. "So, how did you like Ann?"

"Very much. I'm having dinner at her home next week."

"Oh, she and Roger are having another one of their famous parties?"

"No, she invited me over because I'm interested in renting her sister's apartment."

"What?" Kyle looked as though someone had thrown cold water in his face. "You're moving?"

"Yes, but not until the fall." Paige wasn't sure but she thought she detected a look of relief in his large dark eyes. "Nevertheless," she continued breezily, "my furniture and car should arrive from New York sometime next week. It'll make things easier if I've already found an apartment."

"Of course. Does Uncle know of your plans?" Bowls of soup were placed in front of them and they began to eat appreciatively.

"Yes." She paused for a moment to look at him. "Actually," she said, "my spending the summer at Greens Cove and then moving to Austin in the fall was all his idea."

Kyle glanced at her briefly but never stopped eating. "How do you like the soup?"

"It's a delicious surprise." For a second she was thoughtful.

"Peaches," Kyle said, anticipating the question in her eyes. "It's cold peach soup."

"You're kidding."

He shook his head. "Uncle is going to miss you an awful lot when you move."

"Maybe. And just maybe by then he'll be tired of me and the Rindleton Project."

They laughed softly. "Hardly. I know Nathan Buchanan very well, and he's already grown very close to you. He doesn't do that easily."

"Perhaps he sees me as the daughter he never had."

His large dark eyes searched her face. "I hope you're right, but I could never accept you as my aunt."

The warm look in Kyle's eyes and the gentle tone of

his voice threw Paige completely off balance. "What do you mean?" she asked, smiling uncertainly.

"I refuse to explain a couple of simple sentences to a woman with a doctor of philosophy degree from Columbia University." The waiter removed their soup bowls and replaced them with salad plates filled with a colorful mixture of vegetables. "Red lettuce, beans, endive, mushrooms and truffles mixed with a warm goose-liver dressing," Kyle announced. "Enjoy."

For a while they ate in silence taking in the beauty of the valley. "I've never seen a place as lovely as this," Paige said.

"I'm pleased you like it. I bring only very special friends here for very special occasions."

Paige smiled and changed the subject. "When the legislature isn't in session do you get to Austin often?"

"Yes. I come regularly to visit Uncle and to enjoy the hills and the lakes."

Plates of succulent veal chops with chicken-of-the-woods mushrooms and matched green beans now took the place of their empty salad plates. "Mmm, this tastes wonderful, Kyle."

He watched her take several more forkfuls of food into her mouth. "May I assume that I'm slowly but surely redeeming myself with you?"

"You're definitely on the right road," Paige said, "but you have a long way to go before reaching your destination."

"Oh no. I hadn't realized I had blundered that badly. I had planned to be in your good graces by the end of the day." He smiled. "I won't make it, will I?"

"I think not." The remainder of the main course of their dinner was eaten *sans* conversation, and when they had finished they chose a refreshing mint sherbet for dessert.

"I'm not looking for a fight, Paige," Kyle said, breaking their long silence, "however, it's important that I talk to you about Uncle."

Her happy mood began to fade. Why did Kyle want to spoil their lovely lunch with an argument? "All right," she replied reluctantly.

"I still can't understand why he lost control of his car. If he wasn't preoccupied with you at the time, then what happened to him?" He fixed his eyes on her.

Paige remained calm. "Nat and I were not holding hands, kissing or making love to each other in any other way when we had the accident. As a matter of fact, we weren't even talking. I think you'll have to accept his explanation of what happened."

With a deep sigh, Kyle finished his dessert and pushed his dish aside. "I'm afraid for him, Paige," he said. "He's all I have, and the thought of losing Uncle in a freak accident is more than I can handle."

For the first time since she had met him and much to her own surprise, Paige felt sorry for the man sitting across from her. His concern for his uncle was sincere and she knew he deserved to know the truth about the accident, but Paige couldn't bring herself to break the foolish promise she had made. There had to be some way to resolve the problem without losing the trust of Dr. Buchanan.

"Paige, is there something you should tell me?" Kyle's eyes had been glued to her face since the moment he broached the subject of his uncle, and now he watched her as if his life depended on any movement she made. "Did the car malfunction somehow?"

"No," she said, a little too hastily.

"Is he working too hard? Is that why he had the accident? Is he tired?"

Slowly her fingers went to her head and she began to massage her temples rhythmically. "Perhaps he could use a rest."

Kyle slumped in his chair and stared out of the window. "I've been wondering if I should insist that he retire and come to Houston to live with me."

"That would kill him," Paige whispered.

"Another freak accident could also kill him," Kyle said, in the same soft tone.

"You're right," Paige conceded. "But Nat loves his work. You can't take that away from him."

"And I can't sit around and wait for him to hurt himself either."

Paige hadn't known Nathan Buchanan long, but she did realize that taking him away from Huston-Tillotson, his students, his research and the old family mansion nestled among the Texas hills would be the same as putting a bullet through his heart. And what about Magda Winslow? Kyle always seemed to forget his uncle's relationship with her. Why?

"Kyle, your uncle is a vital, productive man with a mind as sharp as yours or mine. It would be wrong for you to ask him to give up his life here in Austin just because you fear he'll have some kind of mishap and hurt himself. Besides, the odds of his having another serious accident like the one yesterday are almost non-existent. You're being awfully selfish and unfair."

"Perhaps, but lately I've noticed he depends on Magda to do things for him he never would have dreamed of her doing a few months ago." His voice betrayed his irritation, and it became clear to Paige that Dr. Buchanan's illness wasn't the only secret he was keeping from his nephew. But why was he reticent about his love for Magda? "He also seems rather dependent on you," Kyle continued, still watching her closely. "Nathan Buchanan is a proud, independent man, Paige. Something is wrong, and he's hiding it from me."

Another fact had surfaced for Paige. Kyle Buchanan was a hard man to reason with once he had his mind set. Still, she was determined to try. "If your uncle has problems, Kyle, I think you should let him work them out for himself."

He nodded his head as if in agreement but appeared to be completely engrossed in thought. Paige wondered if he'd heard the last statement of her argument. "There's one other thing that we need to discuss," he said.

"What's that?"

"Your relationship with my uncle. Are you lovers?"

Though Paige realized Kyle had suspected all along that she and Dr. Buchanan were romantically involved, the bluntness of his question momentarily rendered her speechless. "No, we're not," she said, at last. "We're only good friends."

"Are you sure?"

"I'm positive. I admire and respect Nat and feel that he likes me as well. There's nothing more between us."

"That's good to hear."

"Why? Are you so selfish you don't want your uncle to have any romance in his life?"

"Not with you." He got up from the table and helped her out of her chair.

"He could do worse, you know," Paige said, angrily following him out of the restaurant.

"I'm very much aware of that." They got into the car

and Kyle made his way back to the freeway. "So, if you're not involved with Uncle who are you involved with?" he insisted.

"I don't speak in code either, Kyle. I've told you once I'm not romantically involved with anyone, nor do I care to be."

"That's hard to believe. You're an awfully beautiful woman, Paige."

"So?"

"So I believe some man somewhere has committed himself to you and now you're denying the poor guy."

"That's your problem."

"Yes, it is." His keen dark eyes raked her for an instant. "Where to?"

"Greens Cove."

He smiled. "Not yet. I seem to have stumbled a bit on the road to redemption. I'd better do something to smooth things out. How about a grand tour of Austin?"

"Please yourself, Kyle."

He drove to the heart of the city, which was built on a series of hills flanking the Colorado River. Major streets were peppered with old historical buildings and as they drove they made stops at the Governor's Mansion; the O. Henry Museum, the cottage where the eminent short-story writer William Sydney Porter lived and wrote for ten years; the University of Texas, the state's largest university; and the L.B.J. Library, which housed the public papers of Lyndon Baines Johnson, the thirty-sixth President of the United States. Touring the clean, quaint town helped Paige to forget her anger, and before long she and Kyle were laughing and again engaging in easy conversation.

Afterward, he drove to the State Capitol, the massive, classic statehouse made of Texas pink granite. Sur-

rounding it in the parklike area were state office buildings that had won international architectural prizes.

"I've spent a great deal of time in this building during
the past few years," Kyle said, leading Paige into the
Capitol.

"It's impressive."

"Yes, Texans like to boast that it ranks second in size
only to the National Capitol in Washington, D.C."

They made their way to the center of the building
where the open circular rotunda rose to the top of the
dome. Four floors of the Capitol opened onto it. Paige
listened attentively as Kyle pointed out portraits of the
five presidents of the Republic of Texas and the past
governors of the state. She was distracted, however, by
an attractive woman who walked determinately up to
Kyle and tapped him on the shoulder.

With a look of annoyance shrouding his features,
Kyle turned to face the intruder and, recognizing her
promptly, took the woman in his arms. "What are you
doing here?" he asked.

"Using the reference library. How about you?" She
eyed Paige interestedly.

"Playing tour guide to a newcomer in our town."
Kyle introduced them.

State Representative Janet DuBois was slim, with a
sensual mahogany complexion set off by a classic white
linen suit. Her hair, pulled back and held with an ivory
clip, hung to her shoulders in one black bouncy curl.
Subtle hues of plum makeup accented her comely features. "I know you must be enjoying your work with
Nat," she told Paige, with a smile. "He's a delightful
man." Her demeanor was as warm and gentle as an
evening summer breeze, but Paige could sense a tough

intelligence about her. "By the way, how is he?" she
asked, turning to Kyle. "I haven't seen him in months."

"I'm not sure," he answered. "Uncle had a car accident yesterday and I'm a little worried about him."

"Oh, I'm sorry. Was he seriously hurt?"

"We don't think so. He's undergoing a thorough examination today. Hopefully he's fine."

"I'm sure he is," Janet said, placing her hand on his
forearm. "Don't look so worried." She looked at Paige
as if willing her to sanction her remark.

"I've been trying to convince him of that all afternoon," Paige complied.

Janet DuBois smiled. "I'd like to visit Nat if that's
possible. Could you arrange a convenient time, Kyle?"

"Sure, Janet. Uncle would love to see you. Maybe we
can all get together next week after the close of the last
session of the legislature."

"Speaking of next week and the legislature," Janet
said, "are you ready for the strong opposition you're
going to get against your bill?"

"Yes, but I'll get the votes I'll need for it to pass in the
House."

They exchanged a knowing glance. "I know you will,
Kyle," she said. "You always get your way." Touching
his hand lightly, she started out of the rotunda. "Next
week, then," she told him.

Kyle and Paige continued their tour, taking the elevator to the second floor and the House and Senate
chambers, the governor's reception room and the legis-
lative reference library. Following that, they left the
Capitol.

"One more stop before Greens Cove," Kyle announced, maneuvering the Ferrari out of the city and
up a long string of hills.

The late afternoon sun bathed the countryside in golden rays, highlighting its natural beauty and giving the region the aura of an enchanted land. Nevertheless, each time Paige felt a warm glow of cheerfulness begin to spread through her, it was promptly aborted by thoughts of the discussion she'd had with Kyle at the Glass Dome. Had she been wrong to try and convince him that his uncle was in good health? What if Nat had another accident? In that event, she knew she would have to assume at least part of the blame.

"Mount Bonnell Park," Kyle said, interrupting Paige's musing.

Paige looked about her, puzzled. "Where?" she asked. He had pulled off the highway and parked the car next to an escarpment peppered with trees and thick green shrubbery. On the opposite side of the road was a deep chasm.

"It's this way." He pointed up a flight of stone steps which they climbed along with several others. As they reached the crest, cries of delight could be heard all around them, for the hilltop park sat high above Lake Austin, affording a magnificent view of the city and the hill country.

Paige stood at the stone wall that bordered the bluff. "I've run out of superlatives to describe this part of the country, Kyle," she said, gazing at the boats and water skiers gliding over the river's surface. They were so far above the lake that the skiers looked like miniature dolls riding upon a silver beam. Luxurious homes sat majestically amid the trees on the hillsides.

As they watched the scene below Kyle's arms crept slowly around Paige, pinning her tight against his hard muscular frame. A warm prickling sensation began to move through her and, determined to put an end to his discomposing behavior she turned to face him. Large brown eyes melted into round dark ones and their lips meshed in a succession of warm and tender kisses which left them throbbing with desire. For a moment Paige clung to Kyle resting her head against his chest and gently he caressed her cheek.

"I think I'd like to go back to Greens Cove, now," she said, pulling out of his arms. She began making her way down the steps toward the car.

"Have I destroyed my opportunity to make amends with you?" he asked.

Paige smiled and shook her head. "No. No, you haven't." But as she stole a glance at him she realized that Kyle Buchanan was playing a game that could destroy the plans she had made for her career. He was feigning interest in her in order to put an end to her relationship with his uncle. She wouldn't be caught in his snare, she thought. She wouldn't become his pawn. By using the tactic of avoidance, she would simply outmaneuver him.

CHAPTER 7

Paige emptied a couple of ice trays into a pitcher of limeade and stirred it lazily. She was relieved she had finally completed her morning's work and had a legitimate excuse for not working the remainder of the day. Her concentration on the Rindleton Project had been nil, and there were no signs it would improve. Visiting with Ann would be just the break she needed, Paige thought, filling a glass with the cold citrus drink.

"Oh, Dr. Avalon, there you are. Nat asked me to give these papers to you. Would you mind filing them for him?"

"Of course not, Miss Winslow. And please call me Paige."

"Only if you agree to call me Magda."

"Agreed," Paige smiled. "Would you like some limeade?"

"That would be nice."

Paige filled a second glass and handed it to her. "I hope you like it," she said, "I'm not as good at this as you are."

"Oh, I'm sure it's delicious, Paige. Do you have a minute?" she asked shyly. "I'd like to speak with you alone about something that's been on my mind for some time."

"Certainly, Magda. What is it?"

"Let's find a comfortable place to talk," she said.

Wordlessly, they made their way down the hall to the

library and curled up on opposite ends of one of the
sofas. As Paige watched Magda nervously trace geomet-
ric designs on her glass, fear began to well up in her.

"What's wrong, Magda? Have Nat's eyes grown
worse?"

Magda glanced at Paige and tried to smile. "No, no,
it's nothing like that. Nat's condition is about the same."

"Then, what has you so upset?"

"It's all rather embarrassing," she replied, "but I
have to know, Paige. Are you interested in Nathan?"

Paige stared at her. "What do you mean?"

"I mean are you in love with him?"

"Oh, Magda. Is that what you wanted to talk with me
about?"

"Yes. And please tell me the truth," she whispered.

"I'll tell you the truth if you'll promise to tell me
something."

"All right."

"Exactly what have I done to make you think I'm in
love with Nat?"

"I'm not sure," she said. "I just have this uneasy feeling."

"Relax, Magda. I'm not in love with Nat, but you can
be sure of this, I do love and admire him. He's one of the
most wonderful men I've ever met, and I'm grateful to
have this opportunity to work as his assistant. That's the
truth. I hope you believe me."

"I believe you," Magda said, her eyes reflecting her
relief, "and thank you, Paige, for being honest with
me."

"You know, you have nothing to worry about," Paige
went on, "you're a very attractive woman, Magda, and
Nat is in love with *you.*" She considered her for a mo-

ment and then added, "You make a beautiful couple and I feel awfully lucky to know you both."

"That's a kind thing to say," Magda replied happily. "And for some reason I'm glad you approve."

"Why would anyone disapprove?"

Magda smiled and shook her head. "I don't know. I guess I'm worrying unnecessarily."

"I'm sure you are."

"I . . . I hope when Kyle finds out he won't be angry with us?"

"Why would he be angry?" Paige asked. "And why haven't you told him before now?" Finally, she would find out why Magda and Nathan had kept their love secret.

"It was only by accident Nathan never told Kyle about us," Magda said. "When at last he made up his mind we'd marry, he had his first attack of essential blepharospasm. That changed all his plans, and there was no need to tell Kyle anything. Now, he's trying to push me out of his life. Nathan thinks if we marry, eventually he'd become a burden to me. But I won't leave him, Paige. I love him too much." She wiped tears from her eyes with her fingertips. "Be that as it may," she said on a sigh, "I'm a little afraid Kyle may think I'm not the right woman for his uncle. After all, Nathan is the only family he has, and Kyle is very protective of him."

"Don't concern yourself with Kyle, Magda," Paige said. "He has to learn to let his uncle live his own life."

"You're right, of course. And I'm pleased we've had this little talk. I feel a lot better."

"Good. I hope we can be friends, Magda."

"Oh, Paige, that would make me very happy."

Paige rose from the sofa and went to Dr. Buchanan's

desk and filed the papers. "I'd better get changed," she said. "I'm supposed to meet Ann at her sister's apartment in less than an hour."

"Enjoy your evening."

"Thanks, Magda. I'm sure I will."

Paige pulled on a soft lavender cotton dress and sandals and left Greens Cove for Austin in a taxi. Ann was waiting for her when she arrived at Susan's apartment, and after the grand tour of the place, Paige was satisfied that the large rooms with several skylights and glass walls could easily accommodate all her belongings. She made the necessary arrangements to rent the apartment, and then they went across town to Ann's home.

Dinner with Ann and her husband, Roger, turned out to be just what Paige needed. The thick, succulent steak with all the traditional Texas trimmings was delicious and the Fletchers' carefree life-style made her feel as though she was with friends she'd known for years. Following dinner they relaxed on the deck-top gazebo enjoying the view of the river and the temperate summer evening.

Like an imp contemplating some future caper, Roger turned to his wife with a roguish smile. "What do you say to a party in a couple of weeks, Ann? I think Paige and Mark Washington should be given the opportunity to meet each other."

Ann shook her head thoughtfully. "I don't think your friend Kyle Buchanan would appreciate that."

"You and Kyle?" Roger asked, studying Paige carefully. "I'm sorry. I didn't know."

"There's nothing between Kyle and me," Paige replied.

"But, Paige, he's such a terrific guy," Ann said.

"Wouldn't you like there to be something between you?"

"I hardly know the man, Ann. I don't know if I'd like to get involved with him or not."

"Roger and I can be very helpful there," Ann said. "What information do you need to make your decision?"

"None," Paige chuckled.

"Good. We'll tell you everything we know. Where shall we start, Roger?"

"He was born?"

"Get serious." Ann turned to Paige, "He *was* born, you know," she said with a laugh, "thirty-three years ago. He attended private schools here in Texas and then like his father and uncle earned his degrees from Yale University. After that he moved back to Texas and set up his law practice in Houston which, by now I'm sure you've learned, is very successful."

"Yes, Nat has told me quite a bit about his nephew's accomplishments, especially those he's had in the legislature. I understand he has a very impressive record."

"Mmmm, I think you've hooked her, Ann."

"So I see. Yes, Kyle's done well. I know his father would be proud of him. Philip Buchanan was a Houston city councilman for a number of years. I presume that's how and why Kyle first got interested in politics."

"It's too bad neither of his parents lived to see him succeed."

"You're right, Paige. But he does have Nat, who thinks the world of his nephew."

"Is that it?" Roger asked. "Have we told her all the important stuff?"

"Roger, really. We haven't even touched on the important information yet."

"What's left?"

"His love life, silly. Now, Paige, Kyle goes out with a number of young women, but he's not serious about any of them."

"How do you know?"

"Trust me."

"Fine. I have no intentions of getting close to the man."

"Why not? You and Kyle make a lovely couple. I think you should get to know him, Paige."

"What about Janet DuBois?"

Paige noticed Roger and Ann exchange a quick glance. "Have you met her?" Roger asked.

"Yes, and she's beautiful and obviously very talented."

"Janet and Kyle have been friends a long time, but that's all," Ann assured Paige.

"Forget it," Paige laughed. "I don't need any problems in my life. Things are going very well for me now and I intend to keep it that way."

"No one can say we didn't try, Ann," Roger told his wife.

Paige went from room to room admiring her new apartment. Her furnishings and car had at last arrived from New York and she'd taken great pains in finding just the right spot to place each article of furniture right down to the last miscellaneous trinket. She hadn't thought the antique pieces would have looked so attractive in the ultramodern suite of rooms, but the new and the old complemented each other perfectly. Studying the original Chagall she had inherited from her grandmother which now hung above the fireplace, Paige wondered if Kyle would find her place attractive.

It didn't matter, she decided. No doubt he would never see it.

Paige left her Austin apartment in her metallic blue-gray Porsche with the comforting knowledge she'd have a hideaway when and if she ever wanted or needed a break from Greens Cove.

CHAPTER 8

"You're not coming with us, Paige?" Dr. Buchanan asked.

"No, but thanks for inviting me. I've decided to stay here and work. There's some reading I should get done before we visit Rindleton at the end of the week."

"Nonsense. Exciting things will be going on at the Texas legislature today, and we should all be there to witness them."

"He's right, Paige. And I think you'll find our Texas lawmakers rather interesting to observe."

"That's an understatement if I've ever heard one, Magda. Don't you think we should prepare the young woman for what's sure to happen?"

"Everyone may be on their good behavior, this time, Nathan. There probably won't be any fistfights during this session."

"Fistfights?" Paige asked.

"Sometimes tempers are difficult to keep under control," Dr. Buchanan answered, a trace of a smile on his lips. "Now, Paige," he continued, "put aside the Rindleton Project for today and come with us to the Capitol. I'm sure Kyle would appreciate your interest, and Magda and I would enjoy your company."

Remembering the pledge she'd made herself to avoid Kyle Buchanan, Paige studied the fresh bouquet of daisies that sat in the center of the table. Although she'd been successful in shunning him physically, her thoughts had betrayed her daily. So, how would she ever succeed at putting him out of her mind if she spent the day watching him in the legislature?

"We won't take no for an answer," Dr. Buchanan told Paige, jolting her out of her musing. "We positively insist you come with us."

Paige looked from Magda to Dr. Buchanan. "All right," she said, feeling she had no alternative, "just give me a few minutes to change."

She went to her room and quickly got out of her slacks and shirt. After carefully contemplating her reflection in the mirror, Paige slowly took the pins from the knot at the nape of her neck and brushed her hair until it fell into soft, bouncy waves about her face and shoulders. Although she realized most visitors viewing the proceedings in the House chamber would be casually attired, she decided to wear something dressy. Paige pulled on a long-sleeved silk dusty-rose-and-beige print dress and began pushing tiny covered buttons through the corresponding loops of the moderately low scoop-necked bodice. The fabric hugged her full bosom and the soft gathers of the full skirt clung attractively to her trim hips. Stepping into high-heeled taupe leather sandals and slipping on her chunky gold earrings and bracelet she again moved in front of the mirror. I shouldn't look too out of place, she told herself as her eyes slowly swept her form. For several minutes she was thoughtful. You're foolish, Paige. Why have you dressed to attract Kyle Buchanan's attention when you know he's shown interest in you only to destroy your relationship with his uncle? Have you gone mad and forgotten your plans for your career? Don't play into his hands and ruin your opportunity to work with Nat. Don't fall in love with him, Paige, she pleaded.

"Are you ready, Paige?" Magda asked, knocking softly at her door.

"Yes, yes I am," Paige answered. She took her small taupe leather bag from the bed, slipped the slender strap over her shoulder and stepped into the hall.

"Oh my, how beautiful you look," Magda said. Paige acknowledged her compliment with a smile, and they made their way out of the house and to the garage where Dr. Buchanan waited.

"You look lovely, Paige," he said, adding his compliment to the one already issued.

"Thank you, Nat."

They got into the car and Magda slid behind the wheel of the newly repaired Lincoln. Their conversation, during their twenty-minute drive, was light and cheerful and by the time they arrived at the Capitol, Paige's state of mind had improved.

Upon entering the famous Texas pink granite building they took the elevator to the balcony.

The House chamber was charged with excitement and crowded both with visitors and lawmakers. As Paige looked about the viewing area for vacant seats she spotted Thomas Cox sitting in the center of the last row of chairs in the gallery. Directly below him was Ann Fletcher. She caught Ann's eye and waved just as Dr. Buchanan found three unoccupied chairs in the front row. After taking their seats Paige realized she had allowed the older woman to enter the aisle first and she found herself sitting between Magda and Nathan.

"Oh, Magda, I'm sorry," she said. "Would you like to change places with me?"

"Of course not, Paige. This is fine."

Paige focused her attention on the House floor. A wave of passion rushed through her as she recognized

Kyle talking calmly to a man gesturing wildly. She had never seen him in dress clothes and was a little surprised at how distinguished he looked in his crisp white shirt and steel-gray pinstripe suit.

Magda leaned over the banister and slipped on a pair of glasses. "Who's that at the podium?" she asked, sliding back in her chair.

Dr. Buchanan's gaze went to the front of the room and he studied the man standing there for a moment before chuckling softly. "Are you kidding me, Magda?"

"No, Nathan." Again she moved to the edge of her seat, "He looks familiar—like someone I should know—but I can't place him."

"That's W. K. Johnston, one of our resident boxers."

Magda gasped and pressed her fingers over her lips to stifle a giggle. "I thought I recognized him," she said.

"Looks like things have already gotten rather exciting," Dr. Buchanan told them. "Kyle seems to be trying to talk some sense into Richard Dickenson, one of his aides. I sure hope he gets the votes he needs for his bill to pass without too much hassle."

"What bill is he sponsoring?" Paige asked.

"Kyle wants to create five new district courts for Harris County, which upsets a lot of people."

Surprised, Paige tore her eyes from the young lawyer for the first time since she had spotted him and turned to Dr. Buchanan. "Why? It sounds like a good idea to me."

"The rural legislators don't think it's such a good idea. They're against urban growth and don't want to see those counties become any more powerful than they are."

"I see. Do they present any real threat to Kyle?"

"They can kill his bill. The Texas legislature is dominated by rural legislators."

"I didn't realize that."

"Oh yes, Kyle may have to do some real hard politicking to get that bill passed," Magda added.

Paige returned her attention to the House floor, where Kyle had moved across the room and was holding both hands of and talking with the attractive Janet DuBois. They spoke for several minutes before the state representative, beautifully clad in a light-peach-colored suit and high-heeled dark brown pumps, laughed softly and walked away, her single black curl bouncing as she moved.

Paige watched Janet make her way down an aisle and to her desk where she slipped into a chair and began writing on a note pad. What was her relationship with Kyle? Paige wondered. Were they more than just friends and fellow lawmakers? She sighed silently. Why does it matter, Paige? she asked herself.

"I didn't know you people were here," Thomas Cox said, squatting at the side of Dr. Buchanan.

"Hello, Thomas." The two men shook hands. "We've been here about half an hour now," Dr. Buchanan said, looking at his watch. "How have things been going this morning?"

"Well, there's good news and bad news."

"That's not surprising," Magda commented. "So give us the good news first."

"We got the word earlier this morning that Kyle's bill passed in the Senate."

"That is good news," Paige said.

"Yes, Thomas," Dr. Buchanan agreed, "that has definitely prepared us for the bad news. What is it?"

"I just came from downstairs and understand that

things aren't going well here in the House. Kyle's going to have to do something in order to swing the support of the key representatives, Brady Ford and Carl Stone of Nueces and Starr counties."

Dr. Buchanan looked worried. "Kyle expected a close vote," he said, "but he wasn't anticipating any real problems. Do you know if he has plans to beef up his urban support?"

"Yes, I think he's arranged to talk to both Mark Williams and Juan Perez, the key representatives from Dallas and Bexar counties during the midday break. Right now his strategy is to have a couple of his people filibuster for the next hour or so to keep the bill from coming to a vote before the afternoon session."

"Good," Dr. Buchanan said, the frown slowly melting from his brow. "That'll give him time to do what he has to do."

"Right." Thomas Cox got to his feet. "I'm going to see if I can find out any additional information," he said. "I'll talk with you later, Nat. Goodbye, ladies."

Nathan Buchanan threw up his hand and waved at his friend who had already begun to make his way up some steps and out of the gallery. Before his hand left the air, however, he was forced to take it swiftly to his face to shield his eyes. Paige realized he was having an attack but calmly pretended to watch the scene on the House floor. After several minutes she sensed him relax.

"Are you all right, now?" she asked.

"Yes," he whispered, with a nod, "and thank you, Paige, for your discretion." She smiled and turned unseeing eyes to the activities ahead of her.

"Janet is a good-looking woman, isn't she?" Magda asked Paige, unaware of what had just happened to the man she loved.

"Wh— . . . oh, yes," Paige answered, forcing her
mind back to the proceedings. "Quite charming, too. I
met her last week." Janet DuBois was at the podium
speaking in a clear rich alto voice. She presented her
ideas to her audience with enthusiasm, as if she had the
attention of every lawmaker in the room when, in fact,
no one seemed to be listening to her at all. Her peers
were instead talking to each other in rather loud voices.
Paige heard someone scream "shut up" and turned to
see one man shove another. A smile tugged at the corner of her lips as she shifted in her chair and met Dr.
Buchanan's gaze.

"Let's go and have some lunch before the restaurants
around here get too crowded," he said. "Janet has
things well under control."

Paige and Magda followed Dr. Buchanan out of the
Capitol and a few blocks away to a small Mexican restaurant. Though it was crowded, they were lucky
enough to find a table and order their lunch. As they
washed down spicy tacos with iced sangria, Paige's
thoughts wandered to Kyle and the task he had before
him. Silently, she prayed for his success with the District Courts Bill, not only for his sake but also for the
benefit of his uncle. For as she watched Nathan Buchanan sitting across the table from her she began to
understand that he had wanted to see Kyle at work in
the legislature at this juncture fearing he would never
have the opportunity to observe his nephew in the
Texas Capitol again.

They had been in the restaurant for little more than
an hour when Thomas Cox entered the establishment,
looked about excitedly and then rushed over to their
table.

"Thomas, if we had known you were coming to San

Angel for lunch, too, we would have waited for you,"
Magda said.

"That's all right," Thomas replied. "I've just finished
a cheese sandwich and a cup of coffee. I came here only
because I was looking for Nat." He pulled out a chair
and sat down. "We have nothing more to worry about,"
he announced, turning to Nathan. "Kyle is caucusing
right now with all the key people necessary to pull this
thing off."

"I hope he's able to persuade them to vote in his
favor," Paige said.

"With his personality Kyle can sway most anyone to
do whatever he wishes," Thomas replied. "And besides
that Mark Williams and Juan Perez are in his debt. If it
hadn't been for Kyle, Williams never would have gotten his new junior-college district and Perez would
have lost out on that much needed state hospital for his
county."

Dr. Buchanan snapped his fingers. "That's right. But
how is he going to win the support of Ford and Stone?"

"A beautiful plan is in the works," Thomas smiled.
"Nueces and Starr counties want to purchase water
from Arkansas and have it piped to South Texas for
irrigational purposes."

"Is Kyle in favor of that bill?" Magda asked.

"He's neither for nor against it," Thomas answered.
"But the bill is important because it's not on the
agenda, and Kyle knows the governor is considering
adding two other items to the docket. When he informs
Ford and Stone of this and reminds them of the fact that
he has the governor's ear and is willing to speak with
him about their water project providing he gets their
support for his bill, he'll get his votes."

"All of this is getting so exciting I can hardly stand it," Magda said.

"Yes, it is." Dr. Buchanan got to his feet. "Let's get back to the Capitol before we miss something."

As they walked back to the statehouse Paige realized her earlier notion about Kyle had been accurate. He wielded quite a bit of power in the Texas legislature.

They found seats just as the afternoon session was called to order. A ballot on the District Courts Bill was requested. The 150 state representatives began casting their votes, and it wasn't long before cheers were heard in the gallery.

"I'm so happy for Kyle," Paige said.

"I am too," Dr. Buchanan replied. "From this point on things should be very easy for him with that bill."

They lingered in the gallery of the House of Representatives for a few hours longer watching the remaining proceedings and talking with Thomas Cox, Ann Fletcher and other friends of the Buchanan family before leaving for home. Their departure had been prompted by a message from Kyle delivered by one of his aides saying he would be taking some friends and several of his colleagues to Greens Cove for a victory celebration. Magda decided to prepare a light supper for them and encouraged Paige and Dr. Buchanan to leave Austin immediately.

Once they reached the house, Paige volunteered to help Magda with the meal. The older woman prepared fruit in sauterne; cannelloni, the small rolls of stuffed pasta with the two sauces; and tossed a green salad. Paige readied an elaborate antipasto of cold meats, marinated vegetables, fish and a variety of cheeses. A long table, covered with a white linen cloth, was set up on one side of the spacious wraparound porch and filled with the delicious dishes they had made, along with bread and a chilled dry white wine. As they put the finishing touches on their table a caravan of cars pulled into the driveway and the passengers poured onto the lawn making their way to the porch. The beat of Paige's heart accelerated slightly as she watched Kyle make his way toward them, his suit coat hooked on his forefinger and flung over his shoulder. Janet DuBois was close on his heels as was Thomas Cox. Dr. Buchanan greeted his nephew on the steps of their home with a hug and kisses on both cheeks. "Congratulations, my boy," he said, with a broad smile.

"Thanks, Uncle," Kyle replied, "and I really appreciated your coming to the Capitol today."

"I wouldn't have missed it for anything," Dr. Buchanan told him.

The guests gathered on the porch and introductions were made, after which Magda led them to the food-laden table. After plates had been filled and seats found, the group sent up a light buzz of conversation.

Paige watched Janet DuBois casually slip her arms around Nathan Buchanan's neck, tilt her head back and close her eyes. The historian quickly pecked her on the lips and they both laughed gaily. Disengaging themselves, they walked over to the buffet.

"Have you two ladies met?" he asked.

"Yes, last week at the Capitol," Paige answered. "You were wonderful today, Janet. I understand it was your skillful filibustering that allowed Kyle the time to secure the support he needed for his bill."

"Oh, it was all in a day's work."

"Janet is an adept politician," Dr. Buchanan said. "She and Kyle make a great team."

"Why, thank you Nat," Janet smiled. "I've been trying to convince your nephew of that for years."

Their soft laughter floated out over the lawn and
Paige's heart sank as she allowed a weak smile to curl
her lips. She no longer had to wonder about Janet's
sentiments for Kyle, she thought. The lovely and talented politician had just made her feelings perfectly
clear.

"Aren't you coming around to the front with us?"
Janet asked, when she and Dr. Buchanan had finished
serving themselves.

"Yes," Paige answered. "As soon as I replenish some
of our dishes here, I'll join you."

"Don't take too long, Paige," Dr. Buchanan said, with
a smile and a wink. "I want you to enjoy the party."

"I'll only be a minute." She watched the couple move
down the porch and out of sight and then quickly refilled bowls and platters.

"I understand you helped prepare this meal, Paige,"
Thomas Cox said, refilling his plate. "Everything is delicious."

"I'm glad you're enjoying it, Thomas."

"Why are you still back here?" he asked. "Come on to
the front, the conversation is as satisfying as the food."

"I'm on my way," Paige replied thoughtfully. "Inci-
dentally, what happened to Ann? I thought she was
coming to Greens Cove, too."

"Ann had wanted to come," Thomas said over his
shoulder, "but a stack of papers that needed grading for
tomorrow kept her in Austin."

Paige sighed and turned her attention toward the
hills. She had been feeling let down since the moment
she saw that Ann wasn't with the group Kyle had invited to the victory party. Consequently, feeling friend-

less and alone, Paige poured some wine and sipped it wistfully as she watched nature paint the western sky vivid colors of purple, lavender and pink. "It's a beautiful sunset, isn't it?" Kyle asked. Startled by his sudden appearance, Paige stared blankly at him. "Oh, how I love those beautiful smoky brown eyes," he whispered, moving closer to her.

"Hello, Kyle and congratulations on your victory today."

He took the glass from her fingers and drank from it, his eyes fixed on her face. "I was surprised but very pleased to see you at the Capitol this morning," he said. "For the past few days I'd gotten the distinct feeling you were avoiding me."

The hollows and planes of the young politician's face were highlighted by the last flickering glow of the sun, and Paige couldn't help but admire his handsomeness. "I've been very busy lately," she told him.

He smiled. "I've been rather busy myself," he said, "and I'm happy to see that now we both have a little free time. I've thought of you often."

She nervously reached for her glass, which he returned, and drank thirstily from the slim crystal goblet. "I know why you're doing this," she said, taking a step from him, "but it won't work."

His brow knitted in obvious agitation. "It won't?" he asked.

"No." Paige placed the goblet on the table and stepped back the second time.

"Now, tell me," Kyle said, pursuing her slowly, "what is it that won't work?" Taking both her hands in his, he drew her to him.

"This silly game you're playing of pretending interest

in me when we both know you're only doing it to protect Nat from my supposedly amorous advances."

"Oh, Paige," he said, releasing her, "I thought we'd
been through all of that."

"I did, too." She left the porch by the side steps and
Kyle followed her. "I'm not interested in your games,
Kyle," she said.

"Good, Paige, I'm not interested in games either."
He slipped his arm around her waist and silently they
crossed the lawn to the edge of the woods. "Were you
lying when you told me you and Uncle are not lovers?"
He stopped and turned her to face him.

"No, of course not," she answered, indignantly.

"Then what is this all about?" he asked. "I believed
you then just as I believe you now."

"I don't . . . I don't know," she stammered. Quite
taken aback by the candor with which Kyle had spoken,
Paige pulled away from him and started into the woods.

"We'd better not go any farther," he called softly.
"It's getting too late and too dark."

Paige turned and walked slowly back to where she
had stood a few seconds before. Face to face, their eyes
locked and Kyle's large warm hands stole up to caress
her face. "Thanks for wearing your hair loose and such
a pretty dress, today," he said. "You look more beautiful
than ever." The last rays of the sun had left the sky
softly aglow, allowing just enough light for large round
fawn-colored eyes to first search and then dissolve into
dark warm ones. Tenderly Kyle kissed Paige on the
forehead, the nose and the soft curve of her neck before
passionately claiming her waiting lips. She returned his
kisses helplessly as he molded her slim body to his long
muscular frame.

At last Paige disimprisoned herself from Kyle's embrace. "Your guests are waiting," she said, her body aflame.

"They'll have to leave for Austin shortly," he replied. "Spend some time with me after they've gone."

"Yes," she promised, nodding her head.

They went back to the house, rejoining the group on the front porch, and Paige found herself quickly and smoothly drawn into the conversation. Though the dialogue was stimulating, her attention inadvertently fixed on the dynamics between Kyle and Janet and Janet and Dr. Buchanan. She neither sensed nor observed any romantic interchange between the woman and either man, but still the beautiful and talented politician caused her some uneasiness.

"Now that we've thoroughly discussed national, state and local politics as well as world affairs and solved all the problems of the planet, I think I'll go home and prepare for my morning seminar," Thomas said, getting to his feet.

"Tom, just what are you teaching this semester?" Donald Hale asked. "I heard the sweet sounds of Louis Armstrong's trumpet when I passed your room the other day. I almost joined your class."

Thomas laughed. "You should have," he said. "I'm teaching that course for the first time and the students and I are having a ball. We're doing comparative studies of some of the old jazz greats."

"Mmm, maybe I will stop by when I finish testing my political science class in the morning. Who's on docket?"

"Oh, a mixture of people, I think. Coleman Hawkins, Billie Holiday and probably Andriette Brandon."

"Aah, Andriette Brandon," Dr. Buchanan said, "Mary Ann and I had the privilege of hearing her play many times when we were living in Europe. She is a very kind lady as well as a great musician."

"You met her?" Paige asked. "Gram never told me she knew you." The porch fell silent, bodies pivoted and all eyes focused on her.

"You know the great Andriette?" Kyle asked.

"I didn't mean to create a scene," Paige said self-consciously, "but Andriette Brandon is my grand-mother."

"What?"

"Really?"

"How fantastic."

"Why, Paige, what a wonderful revelation. Mary Ann and I were fortunate enough to be invited to Andriette's elegant homes in Paris and in Rome. She is a grand hostess, you know, and likes giving lavish late-night dinner parties."

"Yes, I know."

"She is an extraordinary woman, Paige. And, a wonderful friend."

Paige nodded as she listened to Nat speak.

The party over, Paige went to the library to meet Kyle. In the dimly lit room, Nathan Buchanan sat on one of the sofas, his head resting in his hands. "Nat?" Paige walked quickly over to where he sat. "Are you all right?" When he didn't answer she slipped her arm around his shoulders. "Nat?" she called softly, "is there anything I can do to help you?"

"No. No, Paige. It's all over now. Please just give me a couple of minutes, and then I'll go up to bed."

Paige considered him for some time before again speaking. "Nat, now that Kyle has gotten his bill through the legislature, talk with him about your illness. He may know a very good doctor who can help you."

"By no means will I tell my nephew my problems," he said, lifting his head briefly from his hands. "And you mustn't tell him either, Paige. Remember, you've promised."

With sadness Paige shifted her attention from the dejected historian to the doorway where her eyes met and held Kyle's gaze. His features contorted with disbelief and anger as he fixed his eyes on her arm draped around his uncle's shoulders. Paige opened her mouth to speak, but he turned quickly on his heels and walked away.

"I'll leave you now, Paige," Nathan Buchanan said, getting to his feet. "Will you please say good night to Kyle for me?"

"Yes . . . yes, I will." She watched him leave the library through tear-filled eyes and after a short while made her way to her room.

Downhearted, Paige changed into her nightgown and crawled into bed; but sleep eluded her. At dawn, exhausted from a restless night she dressed and returned to the library to work.

CHAPTER 9

Paige, leaning against the porch railing, took Steven's letter from her pocket and read it a third time. He was in Houston for a Middle East briefing at the home office of the Roll, Hart and Blair Engineering Company and wanted to see her before returning to New York. Though Paige could have discouraged his visit, she had called his hotel and left a message inviting him to Austin. He was to arrive at Greens Cove late that afternoon.

Studying her feelings carefully, Paige realized she was neither happy nor nervous about their impending meeting, only curious. She wanted to see Steven, for she needed to be sure her decision to pursue her career had been right. Paige wanted to test her emotions and make certain she no longer loved him. And, it would be nice, she thought, to wish him luck with his career. Seeing Steven again would be interesting, Paige decided.

She got to her feet and caught sight of Kyle exercising under the oak tree. Her heart skipped a beat and a lump formed in her throat. Did she really have to test her feelings for Steven? Hardly. Kyle's gaze met hers and, draping a towel around his neck, he made his way to the porch.

"You're up and at 'em awfully early," he said, slipping onto the sofa.

"Good morning, Kyle."

"Did you and Uncle enjoy your rendezvous last night?"

Paige sat back down on the porch railing. "I think that's what I'd agreed to have with you," she said. "But it seems you chose to lurk outside the library door and allow your imagination to run wild."

"I'm sure." His gaze was cold, steely. "So, what are you up to now, more work on the Rindleton Project?"

"For a couple of hours. Then I'm off to Austin."

"Oh? I'm going to the city, too. Would you like a ride? Maybe when we both finish our business there we could have lunch."

"That sounds nice, Kyle, but I'll have to get right back to Greens Cove."

"And more work?"

She toyed with the idea of lying and changed her mind. "No. I've invited a friend from New York to visit. I'll have to be here when he arrives."

Kyle's eyebrows shot up and his eyes narrowed into angry black slits. "Well, you're finally letting the mystery man out of the closet. Will Uncle meet his competition?"

"I won't be a part of this ridiculous conversation any longer," Paige said slipping off the porch railing. "And just for the record, Kyle Buchanan, I'm growing very weary of your nasty accusations."

Kyle bolted to his feet. "And I'm growing weary of your nasty conduct with my uncle," he retaliated. "Leave him alone, Paige."

Paige rushed past him into the house and Kyle followed her. But instead of pursuing her into the library he climbed the stairs, two, three at a time.

Though she tried to concentrate on her work, Paige couldn't control her thoughts. They continuously

wandered from Kyle to Steven and back to Kyle again.
Finally, she put the Rindleton Project aside and left
Greens Cove for Austin.

Sitting at Dr. Buchanan's desk in his office at Huston-
Tillotson, Paige methodically plowed through each
drawer, looking for David Tucker's research paper. After not finding it there, she searched all the bookshelves
and tables in the small room. But that, too, proved
unsuccessful. She had decided to give in to her impulse
to leave when the door opened following a soft knock.
Ann Fletcher stuck her head into the room. "Hi. The
secretary told me you were here. May I come in?" she
asked.

"By all means," Paige answered, her spirits lifting.
"We missed you at Greens Cove last night."

"Thanks," Ann said. She sat in the chair opposite
Paige. "I had planned to be there, but my conscience
just wouldn't allow me to put off grading papers another night. I know I missed a fun party."

"Yes, it was very nice," Paige replied thoughtfully.

"So, what are you doing here?"

"I'm looking for a paper one of Nat's students claims
to have turned in last semester."

"Mmm, that sounds a little fishy to me. Who's the
student?"

"David Tucker. Do you know him?"

"Yes, which sheds a different light on the matter. If
David says he turned in his assignment then you can
bet your life he turned it in. He's a straight-A student."

"Then what could have happened to that paper? Nat
and I have looked all over for it."

"It's probably somewhere among Nat's things at
Greens Cove."

Paige released a long deep sigh. "I guess we'll just have to continue to look," she said.

"Sure. It'll turn up." Ann leaned forward in her chair, mischief dancing in her eyes. "What did you think of Kyle in the legislature yesterday?"

His name sent hot prickly sensations coursing through Paige. And, though she didn't want to, she answered, "I thought he was wonderful."

"Yes, well, have you two gotten together or anything, yet?"

"No, Ann, nothing is happening between us," Paige said, a smile curling her lips. She wondered what Ann would think if she told her just what was going on between the young lawyer and her.

"Oh, shucks." Ann slumped back in her chair. "Roger and I had a little bet that the two of you were probably very good friends by now."

"What?" Paige's eyes were incredulous.

"Oh, please don't misunderstand," Ann said. "We both feel that you're perfect for Kyle and had hoped you two had at least gotten to know each other."

"That's sweet of you Ann, but I doubt if anything of a romantic nature will ever develop between us."

Ann looked disappointed but said nothing more on the subject. And, following her convincing argument, they had lunch together at a small restaurant near the college. Afterward Paige began her drive back to Greens Cove.

Her thoughts centered on Dr. Buchanan and the alleged lost paper. If David Tucker turned it in, and now she believed he had, what could have happened to it? Had Nathan stuck it someplace and forgotten where? That was likely. The historian's eye problem had obviously affected his competence in the classroom as well as his ability to manage his research projects properly. Paige feared if he didn't find help soon his condition would force him out of the teaching profession.

Magda and Nathan were sitting on the porch when Paige arrived and informed them she'd been unable to find the paper. The historian's face grew dark with disappointment and Paige wished she could do or say something to reassure him.

Hurriedly, Magda got to her feet and took Nathan's hands in hers. "Come," she said, with a broad smile, "let's walk. It'll make you feel better."

Nathan hesitantly followed her to the edge of the porch. "Would you care to join us, Paige?" he asked.

"No. I think I'll stay here. I'm expecting my friend, remember?"

"Oh, that's right," he said. "Well, have a nice visit. And thanks, Paige, for all you've done today."

Paige sat on the top step of the porch and watched as they moved down the footpath toward the pond and out of sight. She glanced at her watch. Steven wouldn't arrive for another hour. Feeling a bit restless, she got to her feet and began wandering about the yard. She started to pick some of the daisies that bordered the house but decided she'd like some of the wild flowers that grew down at the lake instead. Hurrying to her room, she changed into plum-colored shorts, sandals and a white cotton knit top and made her way to the lake.

Boats of all kinds were skimming the water's surface as Paige promptly forgot the flowers she had gone for and took a seat in the swing. Enjoying the sights about her, she absently propelled herself gently into the air. She waved at Jessie as he momentarily emerged from the woods, surveyed the area casually and disappeared into the forest once again. Time and purpose escaped Paige's thoughts while she took pleasure in the soothing movements of the swing.

"Hi. I was told I could find you here." Neither his voice nor his presence kindled in Paige the passion that only the mention of Kyle's name had brought about earlier in the day. Her lips pulled into a soft smile and she stopped her swinging.

"Hello, Steven. It's good to see you again."

"Thanks for inviting me to Austin." He moved next to Paige, wanting to sit with her in the swing, but she quickly got to her feet.

"It would probably be a tight squeeze if we both sit here," she said. "Let's go out on the pier. I think you'd be more comfortable there." Steven was at least fifteen pounds lighter than Kyle and Paige knew they could both be comfortable in the swing but she didn't want to encourage him in any way. After taking off his tie and jacket, Steven eased down beside her at the end of the pier. Their legs dangled just above the water.

"This place is beautiful," he said, "but it's terribly isolated. Are you enjoying your work here, Paige?"

She turned to him, her eyes reflecting her answer. "This is my dream job," she replied. "I never thought anything this terrific would happen to me. Yes, Steven, I enjoy my work, I'm thrilled to be working with Nathan and although I haven't started teaching yet, I like the college. I've found my niche and I'm very happy."

"Your mother told me you had made quite a fast adjustment. But I found that rather difficult to believe. I wanted to see how you were doing for myself."

"Mother told you the truth." Paige could sense him growing tense as he shifted uncomfortably beside her.

"Austin is not the city for you, Paige," he went on, his

voice tinged with emotion. "You belong in a place that can offer you more. It's nothing compared to New York or any of the other great cities of the world. How do you expect to survive here?"

"Actually, Steven, it's rather unfair to compare Austin with a big city, but, all the same, I like the life-style it offers."

"You're making a terrible mistake, Paige. Living in a place like this dulls the senses. You can only lose if you remain here any length of time."

Paige forced her lips into a smile as she got up from the pier and hooked her thumbs into the pockets of her shorts. "I have no plans of leaving soon, Steven. And please let's not say things that will hurt each other. Let's stay friends."

"I'm not trying to hurt you," he said, squinting at her, "but I do want to make you think." The late evening sun was bright and he shaded his eyes with his hands. "Although there's nothing you can do about it at the moment, you do have an option. Paige, consider returning to New York in the fall. Maybe then we can both rethink our decisions to go our separate ways."

Paige didn't want to believe what Steven was saying. Had he come all the way to Austin to ask her to give up her career again? Did he think for some reason he could now persuade her to forget her work and follow him to the Middle East? For a moment silence enveloped them. She had changed, Paige thought, but only in the sense that she had fallen in love with another man. "Steven, it's all over between us," she said softly. "Can't we just be friends?"

"Of course we can." He got to his feet and took her hands in his. "And I'm telling you this as a friend. I'd hate to see you destroy yourself, Paige, just because of your foolish pride."

He had succeeded. She was angry. But Paige refused to allow him to enjoy his success. Pulling her fingers from his grip, she asked, "How is the briefing going?"

"Very well. I return to New York tomorrow and leave for the Middle East the following Tuesday."

"Have a safe trip and a successful career, Steven."

"Are you going to consider following through on any of my suggestions?" he asked.

"I'm not going to give up my work and move back to New York, if that's what you mean."

"I see. Have you met someone else, Paige?"

"No." The word exploded from her lips and she avoided his gaze.

"Then I guess there's nothing more to say."

"Won't you stay for dinner? I'd like you to meet Dr. Buchanan and my friend Magda Winslow."

"Thank you, Paige, but I think I'll get back to the airport and take an early flight out."

She wondered if he had detected her lie and felt guilty for not telling him she was in love with someone else. "All right," she said. "I'll walk with you to the house."

Steven picked up his coat and tie just as a boat pulled up at the pier. Janet in a white bikini and Kyle with his tie loosened and his suit jacket thrown over his shoulder hopped ashore. Surprised by their meeting they eyed each other curiously. Finally, Paige made the necessary introductions.

Kyle extended his hand to Steven. "It's good to meet you," he said. "I've been wanting to come face to face with the man in Paige's life for a long time, now. She's quite a woman."

Steven shot Paige a knowing glance. "Yes she is," he replied, "but I'm afraid I'm not the man in her life at the present." His gaze held Kyle's. "I suppose I have you to thank for that."

Kyle shrugged. "No, not me," he said. He looked at Paige. "Perhaps someone else."

Paige was aware of her face growing hot with anger and embarrassment, nevertheless, she remained calm. "You're both out of line," she said. "And I don't appreciate your insinuations or innuendos."

Janet, who had been standing slightly behind Kyle softly cleared her throat. "I just happen to have a chilled bottle of chablis on the *Tiki,*" she said, pointing to her boat. "Why don't we all go aboard and have a drink."

Steven thought for a moment and then answered, "I'd like that."

"Yeah, I would, too." Kyle started for the boat and then turned to Paige. "Aren't you coming?" he asked.

Paige knew both men had accepted Janet's invitation mainly to annoy her, but she didn't want to create a scene. "Yes I am," she said.

Kyle poured the wine while they took seats on the deck of the stern.

"Steven, how long will you be in Austin?" Janet asked.

"A few more hours," he said, "then I return to Houston."

"Why so soon?"

"I'm attending a briefing there for a job I've accepted in the Middle East. I have meetings to attend in the morning."

"A job in the Middle East? How exciting," Janet said.

"I was on holiday in Beirut several years ago and I loved it. How long is your tour of duty?"

"Five years."

"That's a long time. But, I suppose you'll make periodic visits to the States during your term."

"Before visiting Paige today I had thought I would. However, now I can see I'd have no reason to come back here."

"You had planned to visit Paige?" Kyle asked. "At one time you two must have had a very special relationship."

"Yes, we did," Steven answered. "But I've been told what Paige and I once had is all over."

"It's not my business—"

"No, Kyle, it's not," Paige snapped.

"Uh . . . would you care to sail up the coast a piece?" Janet asked. "In a couple of hours the sun will be setting and the view from Emersons Bend will be spectacular."

"I'm sorry, I can't," Paige said. "I really must get back to the house."

"I should start for the airport. Thanks anyway, Janet. It was a lovely idea." Steven slipped into his coat and hung his tie around his neck. "Can I get a cab from the house?" he asked Paige.

"I'm sailing right into town where you can get a limousine to the airport," Janet told him. "Come with me and you'll save a lot of time and money."

Kyle fixed his gaze on Steven and Paige. "Perhaps you shouldn't interfere, Janet," he said. "Steven may have things to say to Paige privately."

"No, no, I don't." His eyes met Paige's briefly. "We've had our say. I think I'd like to take Janet up on her offer." Haltingly Steven walked over to Paige, took her face in his hands and kissed her lightly on the lips. "Goodbye," he said, "and do take care of yourself." "Goodbye, Steven."

Kyle stood with her on the pier as the boat sailed slowly down river out of view. Afterward, Paige went to sit in the swing. The unpleasantness that had punctuated her meeting with Steven had left her feeling light-headed, drained. Nevertheless, her curiosity had been satisfied. She had made the right decision to pursue her career and move to Austin. Following Steven to the Middle East and assuming the roles of housewife and mother would have been a terrible mistake. She needed the challenge of exciting work of her own and Paige realized she had found what she'd been looking for with Nathan Buchanan and Huston-Tillotson College.

"You haven't moved for five minutes," Kyle said, sitting down beside Paige. "I thought I'd better make sure you're all right." She attempted to get up but he held her fast against him. "Stay here with me. We need to talk."

His touch caused her pulse to race. She grew very excited. "There's nothing for us to talk about," she told him.

"Yes there is. I need to know what your feelings are for Steven. Do you love him?"

"That's not your affair."

"You're right. It's not. But I'm interested anyway." Paige met his gaze. "I want to know," he insisted softly.

She sighed and turned away. "Not anymore."

"You loved him once?"

"Yes. We considered marriage." She could feel the muscles in his body constricting.

"What happened?"

"We couldn't agree on how to combine our two careers and thought it best to go our separate ways."

He was silent for a long time. "Your career is everything to you, isn't it?"

"No, Kyle. Not everything. But it is important. I wasn't willing to put aside work that I enjoyed so that Steven could further his own career. And I didn't think it was fair for him to ask me to."

"Of course not."

"You agree?"

His lips pulled into a half smile. "Yes. I think a woman has as much right to a career as a man." He got to his feet and held out his hand to her. "We'd better get up to the house," he said.

CHAPTER 10

The days that followed Steven's visit were difficult for Paige. Eating little and sleeping practically not at all, she concentrated on the Rindleton Project, which she worked on each day until exhaustion demanded she get some rest. And in the wee hours of the morning, tossing and turning restlessly, she struggled to cope with the mixture of emotions that troubled her. Though she no longer loved Steven and their parting had been amiable, for the first time since she'd seen Steven in her New York apartment, Paige realized she'd lost a very good friend. Too, her relationship with Kyle had been destroyed the night of his victory party. Just when it looked as though they had settled their differences the same misunderstanding had again come between them.

And, to compound Paige's unhappiness, circumstances dictated that she spend the next several days in Kyle's Houston home. The time had come for Dr. Buchanan and her to visit Rindleton, Texas, which was fifty miles north of Houston. The historian always lived with his nephew when he did research in the Houston area and had insisted they do so on this occasion, as well. Though Paige had tried to explain to him that she would be more comfortable in a hotel room, he had been adamant about their living arrangements. And now, with Dr. Buchanan and Magda Winslow, she stood ill at ease at the door of Kyle's southwest Houston mansion, wondering what they would have to say to each other.

The housekeeper, Mrs. Stone, showed them in. "Mr. Buchanan has been delayed at his office," she said, "and won't be home for another forty-five minutes or more. Come and have a cool drink and relax before going to your rooms."

They followed her to the end of the hall and entered a huge room furnished with leather and suede sofas and chairs. Both chrome and glass as well as dark wood antique pieces accented the area. When she had poured the iced tea, Mrs. Stone left them, promising to return within twenty minutes.

"Nat, I really think Kyle and I would be much happier if I got a hotel room."

"Don't be foolish, Paige. You're practically a member of the family. Besides, Kyle invited you and Magda here so that you can attend his party Saturday night. He would be insulted if you went to a hotel."

"I can't imagine why you think Kyle wouldn't want you to stay here," Magda added. "There's more than enough room in this house for all of us."

"I know but—"

"No buts, Paige. We've just made a four-hour drive and we're all tired. Let's forget this nonsense and relax."

Veiling her anxiety, Paige slipped the thin double straps of her handbag off her shoulder. "All right," she said, "I have no desire to insult anyone." But she could still see Kyle's face twisted with anger and disbelief the night he saw her comforting his uncle in the library, and though they had managed to be civil to each other that afternoon at the lake, she knew he was still very angry with her.

Mrs. Stone showed first Dr. Buchanan and then Magda to their rooms which were on the same hall of the second floor of the mansion. She then took Paige up a short flight of stairs to a third floor that consisted of two rooms at opposite ends of the corridor. The room that had been made ready for Paige was huge and decorated all in white—carpet, walls, upholstered bed, chairs and furniture. Several crystal vases of fresh salmon-colored roses provided the only splash of color in the area.

"I feel as though I've been segregated from the group," Paige said to Mrs. Stone.

The housekeeper had started out of the room, but she hesitated and smiled shyly at Paige. "Mr. Buchanan wanted you close to him," she replied. "His room is there, directly in front of yours."

"I see."

"Dinner will be served in thirty minutes," Mrs. Stone added. "Mr. Buchanan is on his way."

Paige showered and dressed in high-heeled soft rose-colored leather sandals, a pale rose-and-gray striped handkerchief-linen coatdress and her gray pearls. Slowly, she began to pace the white-carpeted floor trying to decide how she should greet Kyle at dinner. Perhaps she would just act as if nothing had happened, she thought, stopping to fiddle with the roses in one of the vases. A soft knock drew her attention to the door.

"Come in," she called.

Kyle stepped into the room and after staring at Paige for a moment walked over to her. "You look very beautiful," he said. "How are you?"

"Hello, Kyle. I'm doing very well."

"I hope you've found the room to your satisfaction."

"Yes. It's lovely. Thank you."

"Good. I've come to escort you to dinner." She took his arm and they went to the dining room where Dr. Buchanan and Magda were waiting.

"Paige had the silly notion that you didn't want her in your home," Dr. Buchanan said, watching them take their seats. "Will you please straighten out this young woman's thinking, Kyle?"

"Of course, Uncle. What made you think such rubbish, Paige?" Kyle asked coolly.

"I thought perhaps you had misinterpreted my actions again and was angry with me," Paige answered, her tone matching his.

"What could you have possibly done to arouse my wrath?"

"I was kind to your uncle." Their eyes locked and held.

Dr. Buchanan and Magda exchanged glances. "Do you understand any of this, Magda?" he asked.

"No," she answered, shaking her head.

"I don't either." He looked at Kyle and then turned to Paige. "But it seems that something is amiss and it involves me. Would either of you like to clue me in on what's going on?"

"It's nothing, Nat."

"No, Uncle, it's not worth your involving yourself."

"I see. Then are you all through sparring for the present time?"

"I am," Paige answered, "and I feel much better after having had my say."

"Yes, Uncle."

"Excellent. May we have dinner, now? Please."

"By all means," Kyle said.

Mrs. Stone served the dinner of oysters Rockefeller,

braised veal with a tuna-mayonnaise sauce, salad, dry
white wine, fresh peach cake and herb tea.

"Your pearls are beautiful, Paige," Magda said, attempting to establish a light conversation.

"Thank you, Magda. They belonged to my grandmother."

"Aha, Madam Brandon," Kyle injected. "I always rel-
ished visiting her. She used to make me think I could
play piano as well as she did."

Paige eyed him skeptically. "You met Gram, too?"

"Of course."

"Why didn't you tell me?"

"I had planned to tell you all about my visits with
your grandmother my last night at Greens Cove, but
something came up that prevented it. I think you'd
become involved in some of that special research that
you sometimes do."

"Oh, yes, I had. I remember it all very well. But I
have time now and would like to hear all about your
exploits with Gram."

"That's exactly what we had," Kyle chuckled. "I met
your grandmother when I was twelve years old and
went to France to spend the month of June with Uncle
and Aunt Mary Ann. I remember the house she had
there. It was big and beautiful with a courtyard and
plenty of flowers. But the memories I cherish most are
the ones of us playing duet on her yellow grand piano
and the times she took me flying in her light plane over
the French countryside. I was the happiest little boy in
all the world."

"You must have forgotten . . . forgotten . . ." Dr.
Buchanan's hands quickly covered his face. "You must
have forgotten our trip with Jean-Claude," he finally
said, his voice muffled.

"Uncle, what is it? What's the matter?"

Paige and Magda, secretly hoping Kyle would discover his uncle was ill, exchanged glances and with heavy hearts pretended to eat hungrily.

"I'm . . . I'm . . . fine, Kyle. It's just that . . . I'm catching cold and . . . have a tickling in my nose. Go on," he said, "tell them about the trip."

Kyle looked at the two ladies with questioning eyes and they both smiled. "We're waiting," Magda said.

"Madame Brandon talked her friend Jean-Claude into taking us down the Seine River on his barge," Kyle went on. "That was the ultimate experience for a kid from Texas." The young lawyer smiled but the enthusiasm had left his voice. He watched his uncle curiously.

"Andriette has many friends from all walks of life," Dr. Buchanan said, recovering and dabbing at his eyes with his napkin. "And they are all interesting people."

"Your grandmother must be a fantastic woman," Magda told Paige. "Did you ever visit her when she lived in Europe?"

"Twice a year. Every July and Christmas. Gram and I always have wonderful adventures. I miss her very much."

Dr. Buchanan patted her hand. "We all do," he gently said.

They finished dinner and retired to the library. "What's your schedule for the weekend, Uncle?" Kyle asked.

"Tomorrow Paige and I will visit Rindleton and Magda will visit some friends and relatives here in town. After that we're free to celebrate Juneteenth."

"That's the nineteenth of June, Paige," Magda said in way of clarification.

"I know, and I'm very excited about it. Will the celebration go on all day Saturday?"

"All day and all night," Dr. Buchanan answered. "So plan to get a good night's sleep tomorrow night. I want you to enjoy the festivities during the day as well as Kyle's black-tie barbecue Saturday night."

"Black-tie what?"

"Barbecue," Kyle said. Indignation glazed the word. "Don't you think that's a little extreme?"

"No. Remember, we're celebrating Juneteenth, the day slaves in Texas learned they had been freed. I think it most appropriate that we do so in our finest clothes and with the tastiest food available. I trust you brought a suitable dress with you."

"Yes, Nat told me you were giving a formal party, but I had no idea it was going to be a backyard barbecue."

"You're in Texas, Paige," Magda laughed.

Kyle folded his arms across his chest and gazed at the beautiful young woman across from him. "Since you're a historian I suppose we don't have to tell you that the slaves in Texas didn't get word of their emancipation until June 19, 1865."

"Yes, Kyle, I know. President Lincoln issued his Emancipation Proclamation on New Year's Day in 1863," Paige said, as if she was reciting a lesson in grade school. "But the slaves in Texas didn't learn of their freedom until much later."

"Consequently, in Texas, we commemorate our emancipation by giving formal backyard barbecues on Juneteenth." He smiled mischievously.

"It was all so very unjust," Magda added thoughtfully.

Paige got to her feet and the men followed suit. "I've had enough," she said. "I'm going to my room."

"Don't be so sensitive," Kyle told her. "Let's go for a walk and forget our differences, for now."

"That's a first-rate idea, my boy," Dr. Buchanan told his nephew. "You two take a nice long walk and clear the air so that we can all relax and have a good weekend." He smiled and winked at them.

Leaving the house by way of the front door, Paige and Kyle crossed the street to the private park that his house along with five other mansions encircled. The twenty-five-acre tract of land had been constructed reminiscent of the three-dimensional Renaissance gardens of château de Villandry in the Loire Valley in France. Within patterned boxed hedges were flowers that themselves made other patterns. Fountains and trees were strategically placed. Vines made a barrel roof for the promenade and the footpaths were raked into ridged designs.

"So, have you heard from Steven since his visit to Greens Cove?"

"No. And I don't expect to hear from him."

"You will," Kyle said. "The poor guy is in love with you, Paige. I doubt if he's going to give you up without more of a fight."

"There's nothing to fight for," Paige replied. "Steven and I could never be happy together. He knows that. He's a very intelligent man."

"I see. Then, I hope he gets over his pain quickly." Shoving his hands into his pockets, he smiled with self-satisfaction. "How do you like our park?"

"It's beautiful. It reminds me of some of the formal gardens I've seen in the château country of France."

"Yes, that was the general idea when we hired the landscape architect. He did a rather good job of it."

"I agree. So, what about these magnificent houses

that surround it? Was it the general idea of the residents to try and copy the castles of France, also?"

"It looks that way," Kyle said. He took her hand in his. A sudden wave of keen emotion rushed through her fingers and up her arm. "Do you think you could learn to live in a place like this?" He gave her a sidelong glance. "And don't ask me what I mean, Dr. Avalon. I know the question is perfectly clear."

"Certainly, I could get use to it," Paige said, thinking all the while Kyle was up to his old tricks. Paige knew he was holding fast to the belief that she still had plans to seduce and marry his uncle and wished with all her heart he could be told the truth.

"And my house?"

"Your house is lovely but rather large. I think I'd get lost and lonely in it."

"I'm sure you could find a use for every room and piece of furniture if it were filled with children with big beautiful brown eyes like yours and winning personalities like mine."

Paige tried to extricate her fingers from the iron grip of Kyle's hand, but he wouldn't release them. "I need to get back so that I can prepare for my visit to Rindleton tomorrow."

"Fine. I'll take you back. But promise me you'll save Saturday for me."

"Juneteenth?"

"Yes, Dr. Avalon."

"You've got it." Their eyes met and they both smiled.

Paige and Dr. Buchanan followed their hostess and guide, Mrs. Celia Mae Brown down Main Street in Rindleton, Texas. The clean tree-lined street, the hub of the small town, accommodated the bank, post office, a feed store, the volunteer fire department, a doctor's office and numerous other shops and municipal buildings. Although its population numbered only 1,047, Rindleton had become the market and commerce center for the surrounding farm area.

They toured the sawmill, the only form of industry there, and the residential neighborhoods of white frame and brick houses with neatly trimmed yards. They were shown the little red schoolhouse and the small white church that the newly freed black men built so many years before. Still housed there were the original wooden benches and potbellied heaters. Mrs. Brown proudly pointed out that the two structures now bore Texas State historical medallions.

After meeting the mayor, who was a direct descendant of Rindleton's first blacksmith, and receiving a key to the town, Paige and Dr. Buchanan returned to Mrs. Brown's home. They made themselves comfortable in the living room and were served an assortment of finger sandwiches, petits fours and fruit punch.

"We certainly appreciate your assistance and interest in our work," Dr. Buchanan told his hostess. "And we hope you and your fellow townsmen will enjoy reading about their ancestors and themselves when the Rindleton Project is published next year."

"Nat we're all very pleased you've chosen to write about us and our little town," Mrs. Brown said, with a soft southern accent. "Furthermore, we want you and your assistant to feel free to call on us at any time we can be of service to you." She smiled demurely and rearranged her short plump frame in her chair. The pink silk shirtwaist dress she wore highlighted her olive-brown complexion and steel-gray hair, which was pulled back and pinned in a neat bun. A modicum of freckles lay strewn across the bridge of her nose and prominent cheekbones. "And do let me point out to you before I forget it," she went on, running her fingers over the table next to her, "this very piece of furniture was made by Lucas Rindleton himself. He was a cabinetmaker, you know."

Paige almost dropped the glass of punch in her hand, she got to her feet and moved across the room so quickly. "Are you sure, Mrs. Brown?" she asked examining the table closely. "Is there any way we can authenticate it?"

"Oh, yes. Lucas Rindleton marked all of his work with an encompassed R." She removed the lamp from the table top and Dr. Buchanan turned the bottom side up.

"There it is," he said. "His mark is as clear as crystal."

"This is incredible," Paige whispered. "Please, Mrs. Brown, may we take some pictures?"

"Of course you may. But this table is plain compared to some of Rindleton's other work. He did rather ornate carvings on most of the furniture he made. Mrs. Temple, who lives right here in town, has a beautiful Rindleton bed and chifforobe. She inherited them a few years back from her great aunt. Also, you may be interested to know that one of his descendants—I can't remember just how he's related to him—has quite a few pieces of furniture that Rindleton made. He lives in Dallas now. But if you'd like, I'll get his address for you."

"Mrs. Brown, that would be magnificent," Paige said, barely able to contain her excitement. "We'd like to meet both Mrs. Temple and Rindleton's relative in Dallas."

Dr. Buchanan sat the table upright again and Mrs.

Brown placed her lamp back in its center. "If you really search about," she said, "you'd probably find some pieces of Rindleton's work that were made before 1865. The furniture he made while he was still a slave is fast becoming collectors' items."

"Yes, we've discovered that and made tentative plans to travel to Virginia where he practiced his trade so long," Dr. Buchanan said.

"Good. As you must know, for years, Rindleton's master hired him out to make furniture for others in and around Virginia. And although he pocketed a portion of the money Lucas made, old man Rindleton saved the bulk of it for his slave and gave it to him once he was freed. With that money Lucas founded Rindleton, Texas."

"He made a grand investment," Dr. Buchanan said, "and I'm certain he'd be overjoyed if he could see his town today."

"Yes, I think so, too," Mrs. Brown agreed. "We've worked hard to make something of this town and ourselves. So many of our young people have gone on to college and become successful doctors, nurses, lawyers, teachers, ministers, TV reporters and even a Broadway star. Have you ever heard of Elise Archer?"

"The star of *Morning's Coming?*" Paige asked.

"Yes. Her roots are planted deep right here in Rindleton."

"That's wonderful. I'd like to interview her. You've given us some invaluable information and leads," Paige said.

Mrs. Brown laughed softly. "I'm enjoying this immensely, and whenever I can be of help to you don't fail to contact me."

"We will. You've already helped us far more than you

realize or we anticipated. We will always be indebted to you, Mrs. Brown." Dr. Buchanan got to his feet. "Now, Paige, I think we should go. We don't want to wear welcome out."

"You're right Nat, but I'm having such a terrific time I hate to leave." After gathering up her belongings she walked over to the mantel where several objects of art were displayed.

"Go ahead and ask," Mrs. Brown said, when Paige hesitated in front of a small slate board.

She turned to her hostess with questioning eyes. "Does it have something to do with Lucas Rindleton?"

"Absolutely not," Mrs. Brown chuckled. "On that slate board my great-grandfather proposed marriage to my great-grandmother." Paige's quizzical expression didn't change and Dr. Buchanan joined Mrs. Brown in her laughter. "Before the turn of the century, Paige, when young men went to the home of young ladies to court them, they did so by what was called 'passing the slate.' Often the whole family, parents and siblings, would be gathered in the living room when the young man came to call and would remain there for the entire evening. Sometimes several sisters would have suitors visiting at the same time. And so, the young men and young ladies communicated privately with each other by writing on slates and passing them back and forth."

"That's the most incredible thing I've ever heard," Paige said.

"What's even more incredible," Dr. Buchanan replied, "is occasionally a young man would have a change of heart and stop passing the slate to one young lady and start passing it to another."

"That took guts," Mrs. Brown laughed.

"It did indeed," Dr. Buchanan agreed.

Saturday. Juneteenth. In navy blue short shorts, matching sandals and a white shirt, Paige sat next to Kyle as he guided his sports car through the early morning traffic of the city. She had brushed her hair, leaving it loose about her shoulders and, paying particular attention to her large brown eyes, had lightly made up her face. She nervously fumbled with the buttons of the blouse she wore, actively trying to quell the growing fondness she was feeling for the handsome young lawyer beside her. Why was she succumbing to his charm, his intelligence, his affection? Why had she allowed herself to fall in love with Kyle Buchanan?

Their first stop for the day was downtown Houston and the Juneteenth parade. Thousands of people lined the streets to watch the elaborately decorated floats, high school and college marching bands, and carloads of politicians move along in the long and colorful procession. On one float was Miss Juneteenth of Texas, a strikingly beautiful young woman with a cocoa brown complexion and short curly black hair. Other floats carried members of her court and depicted scenes of historical moments in the lives of black Americans.

After the parade, Paige and Kyle tried to make their way quickly through the crowd and to the car but were stopped on several occasions. Though Kyle had attempted to keep a low profile by wearing casual clothes —white shorts, a yellow shirt and oversized sunglasses —he had been immediately recognized. The young politician therefore took time to speak and shake hands with those who approached him.

They went to Hermann Park where they enjoyed the music of a Zydeco Band and several performers featured in the annual Juneteenth Blues Festival before going across town to the Juneteenth Arts and Crafts Summerfest on San Jacinto Street where arts and crafts, barbecue, crawfish and soul food were being sold.

Their last stop was made at Adair Park for the annual Juneteenth Down Home Cook-off of greens, fried chicken, red beans and rice, barbecue, seafood gumbo and regular gumbo. Judges for the contest were sports celebrities, local restaurant owners and food experts. Paige and Kyle managed to sample quite a bit of the bill of fare before moving on across the park where a variety of sports were being played. They joined first a game of volleyball and later a touch football match. And before leaving the park they viewed the display of winning entries in the Juneteenth—A Texas Tradition art contest as well as demonstrations in roping and animal care by area trail riders.

When they returned to Kyle's home Paige went directly to her room for a short rest. Nevertheless, it wasn't long before she was up again and dressing for her host's annual formal Juneteenth barbecue.

After a relaxing bubble bath and a brisk massage with a creamy floral-scented lotion, Paige slipped on a long red silk-jersey gown with spaghetti straps that skimmed her body seductively and allowed only a hint of her matching high-heeled sandals to peek from beneath its hem. Opening her jewelry case, she gazed at the ruby-and-diamond necklace and earrings that she had inherited from her grandmother, wondering all the while what Kyle's reaction would be if she decided to wear them. Suddenly she smiled to herself. Intimidating Kyle was one worry Paige didn't have. His parents had been exceptionally successful real estate brokers and had left their only son financially secure. His home was stately, beautiful and furnished in a distinguished manner. Splendid works of art graced the many rooms of his mansion. Not only that, but Kyle, himself, was a success. His self-esteem couldn't be threatened by a few glittering trinkets.

She slipped the gems on and stepped in front of the mirror. Studying herself for a moment she pulled her hair straight back from her face, knotted it and then accented her eyes a little more heavily than usual.

There were two matters that Paige desperately wanted cleared up with Kyle Buchanan before leaving his home this weekend. First, she wanted him to know that his uncle was seriously ill and in need of special medical help. How Paige wished that Dr. Buchanan hadn't been able to camouflage the attack he'd had at dinner a couple of nights before. She would have been able to explain everything to Kyle, then. And secondly, she wanted him informed of the relationship between his uncle and Magda Winslow. Surely if he observed them a little more closely, he would see how very much they loved each other. Once those problems were in the open, Paige felt certain she and Kyle would resolve their differences. And she wanted their differences resolved, because only then could she find out how Kyle truly felt about her. Deep in her heart, Paige hoped his amorous overtures had been sincere. She hoped he was falling in love, too.

After making her way downstairs, Paige stood at the hall door and observed the 150 to 200 guests who wandered gaily about the spacious terrace and the sizable undulating backyard. They looked like representatives from the United Nations, so varied were their features and skin colors. Although most were beautifully attired in customary formal clothes—long dresses, exquisite jewelry and tuxedos—others proudly wore garb native to the countries of their ancestors.

Paige moved through the crowd and into the backyard where the heady smell of hot charcoal and roasting meat drew her to an area where men in chefs' hats worked industriously over spits of Rock Cornish game hens roasting over an open fire. As she drew closer she could see juice bubbling beneath the golden-brown and crackly skins and the fragrance of thyme and tarragon was deliciously intoxicating. Next to that were fresh bluefish barbecuing on hinged grills. On a table a few feet away was the balance of the meal, which consisted of stuffed bread, baked clams oregano, roasted corn on the cob, French potato salad, buckwheat groats with pine nuts, cucumber and tomato slices with sour cream dressing, dry white wine, walnut shortbread, zabaglione, fresh fruit and coffee.

"I hope everything meets with your approval," Kyle said, coming to stand beside her. He was so handsome in his tuxedo he almost took her breath away.

"I must confess I'm rather surprised," Paige replied. "It's all very elegant. The setting, the people, the food, the host." She allowed her voice to trail off.

"Yes," Kyle said, glancing about him, "and yet you outdazzle it all. You do more for red than it deserves."

Paige smiled. "You're kind," she said.

"I'm truthful," he countered. "Now, allow me to sample your charms by dancing with me." He took Paige by the hand and led her to the terrace where a combo was playing popular old love songs. Kyle's compliment had made her aware of herself and she was now conscious of heads turning as they danced. "You see, I'm not the only one who thinks you're beautiful," he told her. Resting her head on his shoulder she allowed him to mold her body to his as they swayed with the flow of the music.

It wasn't until the combo stopped for a short break that Kyle introduced Paige to some of his guests, many of whom were anxious to dance with her. And although he graciously encouraged them, Paige was aware of the fact that his eyes never left her and her various partners for a moment.

The party progressed and Janet DuBois arrived, elegant in white chiffon and pearls. She immediately made her way over to where Paige and Kyle stood talking with a small gathering. With skill, Janet quickly maneuvered the conversation to Texas politics and gained control of the group. Paige, feeling inadequate and left out, excused herself and, noticing Dr. Buchanan at the buffet, went across the lawn to him.

"You're looking awfully handsome, stranger," she told him. "Are you enjoying Juneteenth?"

Laughing, Dr. Buchanan embraced Paige and kissed her forehead. "I can tell you've been spending a lot of time with my nephew," he said. "You're becoming a little tease. And a very beautiful one at that."

"Thank you, Nat. Where's Magda?"

"She's there," he said pointing. "Fill your plate and join us."

"I will." Several dozen small tables covered with white linen cloths were arranged at the left edge of the terrace. Red lanterns sat in their centers. Most were occupied and it took Paige several minutes before spotting Magda and Dr. Buchanan. "You're stunning, Magda," she said, slipping into the chair next to her.

The older woman, dressed in a black silk strapless gown and diamond earrings and pendant, smiled. "You are, too," she replied.

Several others joined them and before long, soft laughter and conversation engulfed their table. Intermittently they danced. And now, Paige, in the arms of the mayor of Houston, moved gracefully around the dance floor. As they whirled to the music, she caught sight of Kyle, who was draped in a chair at a table with a couple of other men. His eyes were fixed on her.

The music ended and the mayor escorted Paige back to the table. As they resumed their eating and conversation, Magda and Dr. Buchanan went to the terrace to dance. Paige watched as they wrapped their arms around each other and smiled. Never losing the beat, Dr. Buchanan kissed Magda's nose, her eyelids and then her lips. He whispered in her ear while his large hands roamed her back and neck. They made an attractive couple and looked happy and very much in love.

Finally, Paige thought, it's happening and all so perfectly. This minute, Kyle could plainly see how completely his uncle and Magda Winslow loved each other. In all fairness, he could no longer accuse her of having a liaison with the historian. For Dr. Buchanan's love for Magda was now in the open. The whole world could see that he and the lovely woman in his arms were in love. One problem solved and one to go, Paige thought.

Surreptitiously, she glanced in Kyle's direction but saw no one. She turned full face and boldly gazed at the table where he had sat. The chairs were empty. She looked about frantically, but Kyle was nowhere in sight.

"Where is he?" Paige shouted. She bolted to her feet with lightning speed and tripped on the hem of her dress. The pull on the soft fabric was so abrupt and vigorous the delicate straps snapped. But Paige didn't really notice. She jerked up a handful of red silk jersey with one hand and stormed about the yard, the terrace and into the house.

"So! There you are," she screamed. Janet, Kyle and the two men who had been at the table with him were standing in the hall having, what appeared to be, a very serious conversation. "Why aren't you ever where you're supposed to be?" Paige demanded. She was so angry her breath came deep and fast.

"Paige, what's the matter?" Kyle asked gently.

"Why is it you never see what you're supposed to see?" she bellowed. "And when you do accidentally open your eyes what you think you're looking at is only a figment of your imagination." Kyle stared at her, his mouth ajar. "Aren't you a lawyer?" she questioned. He tried to speak, but his lips refused to cooperate. "Answer me!"

"Yes, I'm . . . a lawyer," he answered, "but . . . Paige, your dr . . . dress."

At least twenty-five to thirty people had crowded into the hall to investigate the commotion. Among them were Dr. Buchanan and Magda Winslow. Stunned, they gaped at the beautiful young woman.

"You're the most unobservant lawyer I've ever met," Paige yelled, shaking the meat she still held in her hand at his face. Detached crispy golden-brown bits of its skin flew about wildly in the air.

The more she talked the angrier she became, and the more she had to gasp for air. Each time she took a deep breath the bodice of her dress slipped exposing more and more of her full creamy-bronze breasts.

"Please, Paige . . . calm . . . calm down."

"Don't tell me to calm down," she shrieked, and her dress slipped a little bit more. "You've accused me of every filthy thing you could think of and now—"

"Your dress, please—your dress." Kyle dared to inch toward her.

"If you take another step, Kyle Buchanan," she warned, barely getting the words out, "I'm going to scream." She gasped for air and her dress slipped again. Like an exquisite bronze statue draped in red silk jersey, Paige, for a second, stood motionless gazing at Kyle. Then, without warning, she fainted. But before she hit the floor, Kyle scooped her up in his arms and hastily carried her up the stairs.

Paige regained consciousness in the white bedroom with Kyle holding a cold compress to her forehead. "Feeling better?" he asked soothingly.

Staring into space, she remained motionless and silent. Dr. Buchanan and Magda Winslow, carrying a decanter of brandy and glasses, came quietly into the room.

"How is she?" Magda asked in a whisper.

"Better, I think," Kyle told her.

"We thought maybe some brandy would help," Dr. Buchanan said. He poured some of the rich dark liquid into a snifter and handed it to his nephew.

"Try and take some, Paige," Kyle encouraged, but she neither moved nor spoke.

"If you'd like to go back to your guests, Kyle, Magda and I can stay here with Paige until she's feeling better," Dr. Buchanan offered.

"Frankly, I'd like the contrary, Uncle. Would you and Magda mind?"

"No, of course not."

They left them, and Kyle, pouring a brandy for himself, eased down on the side of the bed. With his free hand he slowly stroked Paige's face, arm and back. Desire, deep at her core, began to stir and she had to put an end to the disquieting effect his caresses were having on her emotions. Abruptly she sat up, holding the remnants of the red silk gown tight around her.

"I thought the brandy was for me," she said softly.

"Hi." Kyle smiled at her uncertainly. "I was beginning to get worried about you." Gulping down his drink, he refilled his glass.

"Don't waste your time. I'm fine. But why are you drinking so much?"

"I can assure you I'm in shock," Kyle told her. "I'm still trying to recover from the sudden and violent blow I just received to my sensibilities."

She shot him an icy glare. "Go back to your party, Kyle. I wouldn't want your guests to think you're stuck up here with a hysterical woman."

"Why not? It's the truth, isn't it?"

"I'm all better now."

"I don't think so. You need to tell me what I've done to make you so angry."

"You've falsely accused me of having an affair with your uncle."

Kyle looked at her incredulously. "I thought we had agreed to put those differences aside for the weekend."

"Yes. We had." Her voice was muted and traced with defeat.

"Besides, what does that have to do with that fit of anger you just had?"

Everything, she screamed silently. Paige yearned to tell Kyle she was angry because he had failed to recognize that his uncle had acted strangely at dinner a couple of nights ago because he was seriously ill. Also, she wanted him to see for himself that Dr. Buchanan and Magda were in love. Kyle had missed both opportunities to clear up their misunderstanding, and they were back where they had started. He continued to believe that she and his uncle were romantically involved. Nevertheless, Paige realized she couldn't break the promise she'd made to Dr. Buchanan.

"Nothing," she answered, at last.

"What was it you wanted me to see?"

"I don't know," she said. "Perhaps you were right all along. I'm slowly going mad because I'm working too hard."

He put his glass aside and slipped his arms around her. "Dear sweet, Paige," he said, "you're tired and need some rest. If I leave you now will you try to get to sleep?"

"Sure. I'm fine. And I'm sorry, Kyle. I really didn't mean to embarrass you or upset your guests."

"You needn't apologize," he whispered. "I understand."

For a moment her large brown eyes searched his face. You don't, she thought sadly. You don't understand at all.

Holding her face in his hands, he kissed her deeply and tenderly. "I suppose neither of us will ever forget your first Juneteenth celebration," he told her.

Paige smiled. "No, I suppose we won't," she agreed.

CHAPTER 11

He appeared so unhappy she couldn't bear to look at him.

"Well, how does it feel to be home?" Dr. Buchanan asked. "We've missed you an awful lot around here."

"It feels great, Nat," Paige answered, delighted he considered her part of his family, "especially with the information that I managed to get in Rindleton and Dallas."

"Yes, those were some invaluable leads Mrs. Brown gave us and I appreciate your enthusiasm in following through on them."

"The Rindleton Project is going to be a wonderful chronicle of an extraordinary human effort."

"Thanks to you, Paige, it's going to be just that." Dr. Buchanan smiled and winked at her. "Now, is it too soon to make plans for your trip to Virginia?"

"No. As a matter of fact I had wanted to talk with you about it. I think I'd like to go there around the first of August and stay at least a couple of weeks."

"That sounds perfect and I know this Virginia trip will be as productive as the trips you've just made."

"I hope so, Nat." Paige smiled.

Paige and Dr. Buchanan, taking their usual after-lunch walk, strolled along the path that edged the pond. July had emerged hot as well as dry and the water level of the large placid pool was low. Paige couldn't help but note the drought had robbed the still body of water of its cool and tranquil beauty. Even the distant rolling hills looked withered and dull. But, she was pleased to see that Jessie had kept the lawn and flowers watered, for they were flourishing and attractive.

"I guess I should bring you up to date on the David Tucker problem," Nathan said, clasping his hands behind him.

"You've found his paper?"

"I'm afraid not. And I feel terrible that I haven't. David says the report was over a hundred pages long and I'm sure his research was extensive."

"Didn't he make a copy of it, Nat? A paper that has taken that much work should always be duplicated before it's submitted."

"David had trouble getting his report typed but he gave it to me, the day it was due, just before I left the college for home. He didn't have time to copy it. However, more important than that, I now remember receiving his assignment. He put it in my hands at the exact moment I had my first attack of essential blepharospasm. Paige, I don't know what happened to the paper after that."

"Oh, Nat, what are you going to do?"

"Of course it would be unfair of me to ask him to rewrite his report, now," he said. "Besides, he wouldn't have the time. He's working a full time job and is carrying a maximum schedule in summer school. So, I got him to agree to take an oral exam on his research topic next month. Nevertheless, David's terribly disappointed his paper was lost."

"I know, Nat. But I'm glad you were able to work things out."

"Yes, I am, too."

Halfway around the pond they left the path, walking

a short distance away to a wild plum orchard. The stubby branches of the trees were heavy with the yellow and red fruit and after gathering as many plums as they could comfortably carry in their hands they resumed their stroll.

"There's one other thing that I'd like to talk with you about, Paige."

"Certainly, Nat. What is it?"

"It's Magda. Would you happen to know the reasons why she's been so unhappy lately? Has she mentioned anything to you since you've been back? I've tried to talk with her about her blue mood but she insists nothing is the matter."

Paige looked confused. "No, Nat, I don't. But this morning I did notice Magda seemed upset about something. At first I thought she was angry with me, but when I was unable to determine what I could have possibly done to offend her I decided either my imagination was playing tricks on me or she has grown more worried about your eyes."

"No, Paige, I'm almost certain it's neither your imagination nor my eyes. But something has Magda deeply troubled, and I must find out exactly what's bothering her."

"Do you remember when she started acting this way?" Paige asked, growing more concerned about her friend.

Dr. Buchanan was thoughtful for a moment. "Perhaps a day or two after you left for Rindleton and Dallas. I'm not sure. Nevertheless, I'm worried about her. Please, Paige, try to get Magda to tell you why she's so unhappy."

"I'll see what I can do, Nat."

In a thoughtful silence, Paige and Dr. Buchanan ar-

rived at their starting point and just as they were about
to take leave of the path the historian dropped the fruit
he was carrying and calmly covered his eyes with his
hands. Inadvertently, Paige stepped on one of the
plums and fell against him, sending the historian tum-
bling down the embankment and into the pond.

Her frantic screams, as she scrambled down after
him, brought Jessie out of the woods and to her aid.
Together they pulled the floundering Dr. Buchanan out
of the water and up to safety. After resting for a moment Paige and Jessie helped him to the house.

"What have you done to Nathan, Paige?" Magda
cried out as they entered the hallway.

"Now, now, Magda," Dr. Buchanan said, taken aback
by her tone and accusation. "We had a little mishap, but
we're all right. Paige and Jessie saved my life."

"It seems that every time Paige is alone with you
something terrible happens. I think you should stay
away from her, Nathan."

Stunned, the trio, wet and dirty from their ordeal,
stared at Magda. Seemingly, they were afraid to move
for fear that any motion they made would trigger another effusion of allegations.

At last, Dr. Buchanan dared to speak. His voice was
low and soothing. "There's no need to talk that way,
Magda. Paige has done nothing to deliberately hurt
me."

"I'm sure she's the cause of your little mishap. And I
find it strange that you're trying to protect her." Giving
Paige an angry glance, she took the historian by the
arm. "Come, Jessie, help me get Nat upstairs."

"I don't need any help, Magda," Dr. Buchanan said,
his temper flaring. "And I dislike what you're saying
about Paige. You're being terribly unfair."

"Magda, why are you saying these awful things?" Paige asked, her large eyes filling with tears. "I would never do anything to hurt Nat."

"No, I suppose you wouldn't," the older woman hissed over her shoulder. "You wouldn't do anything to ruin your own plans."

Dr. Buchanan took Paige by the hand. "I'm sorry," he said. "I don't have the faintest idea of what this is all about." With sadness he began to ascend the stairs and halfway up he stopped and turned to Paige and Jessie. "Thank you for saving my life," he added. Reaching the top of the stairs, he disappeared down the hall. Magda followed close behind him.

Completely confused, Paige brushed the tears from her eyes with her fingers and started to her room. Remembering Jessie was standing there, she turned to him.

"Thank you, Jessie. I never would have managed down at the pond without you." Smiling he bowed his head and left.

After deciding not to return to work, Paige showered and pulled on a pair of green shorts and striped green-and-white shirt. She stood on her balcony studying the vast green hills in the distance and trying to understand Magda's curious behavior. Finally, Paige decided that Magda really wasn't angry with her at all. The woman had obviously been under a lot of stress lately and vented her frustrations on the first person to come along. Unfortunately, that happened to be Paige. Feeling better after reaching this conclusion, Paige made her way down the hall to Dr. Buchanan's room. The door was open and Paige went inside.

"How are you feeling, Nat?" she asked.

"Fine," he answered. "A hot bath and a glass of iced tea were just what I needed. Now, I'm as good as new."

"That's great," Paige smiled.

His brow furrowed. "How are you?" he asked.

"I'm fine, too," Paige replied. "And don't worry about Magda, Nat. I'm sure she said all those things because she's upset about other matters. She only lashed out at me because I was there. I'm sure in time she'll talk with you about whatever it is that disturbs her."

Dr. Buchanan sighed audibly. "You know, you're probably right," he said, with a look of relief. "I'm glad you came by, Paige. You've thrown a different light on the situation. We'll just have to be patient with Magda until she works out her problem."

"Yes. I agree." Paige went over to where Dr. Buchanan was sitting by the window and kissed him lightly on the cheek. "Have a good rest," she said. "And by the way, I'm taking the balance of the day off, too."

"Good girl."

They were still laughing when Magda entered the room. "I was just leaving, Magda," Paige said, quickly making her way to the door. "I just wanted to make sure Nat was all right."

Paige left the house and after wandering about in the woods at length found herself down at the lake. Curling up in the shade of the giant pecan tree, she watched the sailboats and water skiers glide by. Before long her tranquil surroundings had lulled her to sleep. It was Kyle's deep and probing kiss that finally roused her.

"That was presumptuous of you," Paige said, her eyes searching his face.

"On the contrary, it was presumptuous of you to think any red-blooded man could resist the temptation of such a beautiful and alluring sight." Kyle took her face in his hands. "Falling asleep so far away from the house and alone was a very naïve and dangerous thing to do, Paige," he said, "and don't ever let it happen again. Something hideous could have happened to you."

She pulled out of his grip. "You're right. I'll be more careful next time."

"Good," Kyle said, arranging himself next to her. "I missed you while you were away researching old Lucas Rindleton. Was your trip profitable?"

"It was perfect. Nat was very pleased with the information I was able to dig up."

"Still making points with the old man, huh?"

"I hope so."

Their eyes locked. "It's still my aim to stop you, you know."

"A waste of time, Kyle. Make plans for a fight. You'll never have the need to use them."

"I desperately want to believe you, Paige."

She stared into the distance. "Did Nat tell you we had an accident this afternoon?"

"Yes and I'm exceedingly grateful to you and Jessie for saving his life."

"Before offering me your eternal gratitude I think you should know my clumsiness caused our little mishap."

"Uncle told me everything, and I'm still terribly thankful to you and Jessie, Paige."

Her eyes scrutinized his face anxiously. "Everything?" she asked.

"Yes. You slipped on the plums he dropped and accidently knocked him into the pond." He met her gaze curiously. "That is what happened isn't it?"

"Certainly." For a few seconds she was thoughtful. "Did he mention Magda to you? She's been acting awfully unhappy lately, and he's deeply concerned about her."

"Uncle mentioned Magda was worried about something, but I don't have an inkling of what's troubling her. I'm sure she'll confide in him when she's ready."

"Yes, I'm sure she will." Paige smiled and rested her chin on her drawn-up knees.

"Don't look so worried," Kyle said, pulling Paige into his arms. He kissed her lightly on the mouth. She returned his kiss. Startled, he studied her face and realized that her eyes encouraged him. With bedewed fiery lips he worked his way to her ear lobe, neck, shoulders and finally stopped to feast at her soft bronze bosom. As her small shaky hands clutched him tight against her, Kyle's hot moist lips rendered Paige molten and forced soft gasping sounds from her lips.

"Mr. Kyle," Jessie called softly from the edge of the woods, "the governor's secretary is on the phone. She'd like to speak with you right away."

Moments passed before Kyle reluctantly disentangled himself from Paige's arms. "Okay, Jessie. I'll be right there." His eyes lingered on Paige before he gave her several brief kisses on the lips. "You were almost a goner," he said, helping her to her feet. "You'd better thank your lucky stars Marie needs to talk with me."

"You were almost a goner yourself," Paige countered. "You're the lucky one."

Holding Paige snug against him, Kyle chuckled lightly. "Dr. Paige Avalon, you're really something special," he whispered.

Paige smiled and pecked him on the cheek. "You are too," she said.

CHAPTER 12

Paige lay awake listening to the steady ticking of the white porcelain clock on the nightstand. All of a sudden it chimed twice. Two o'clock, she thought wistfully. Why can't I fall asleep? She turned onto her back and stared up at the ceiling realizing there were a number of reasons why she was still too agitated to rest.

Magda was still noticeably angry about something. Although she was always polite to Paige, the older woman remained cold and distant. On a couple of occasions, Paige noticed Magda looking at her with eyes filled with painful disbelief and wondered what she had done to elicit such a gaze. Paige even pleaded with Magda to talk with her, but to no avail. Since her flare-up the day of the accident at the pond, Magda had spoken no more than a dozen words to her. The situation was almost unbearable.

Besides that, Dr. Buchanan was slowly becoming a recluse. Fearing his nephew would discover his illness, he began taking his meals and working in his room. The burden of convincing Kyle that the historian was perfectly all right but preferred privacy because of his heavy workload was left up to Paige and Magda. Paige knew Kyle was growing suspicious of their excuses and wished more than ever that she could be candid with him.

She slipped out of bed and pulled on the soft white cotton bathrobe that matched her nightgown. There was still another difficulty that had her unsettled. Kyle Buchanan. She loved him. It was as simple as that. But he didn't trust her, and at the present time there was nothing she could do about it.

Taking the binoculars from the secretary bookcase, Paige unlocked the french doors and stepped out on the balcony. The night was warm and still. The waning moon spilled little light on the yard and countryside. Paige focused the glasses and looked about but saw nothing. Restless, she slumped over the railing and allowed her thoughts to roam aimlessly. Just a few more days, she thought, and I leave for Virginia. Perhaps when I come back after two weeks the air will have cleared and things will be back to normal. Just as she was about to return to her room, Paige glimpsed a spark of light directly under the spreading oak tree. She stopped in her tracks and waited. Another spark. Was someone out there and trying to start a fire? Paige strained to pierce the darkness with the binoculars but was unsuccessful. Suddenly the uncanny feeling that someone was watching her sent cold shivers racing up and down her spine and on shaky legs she rushed into her room and locked the door.

Paige sat on the side of the bed and tried to calm her wildly pounding heart. It wasn't your imagination, she told herself. Someone was out there and unfortunately that someone saw you. When her breathing returned to normal, Paige got to her feet and went to the bedroom door. Opening it slightly, she crept into the hall and slowly began making her way to Kyle's room, thankful he had decided to remain at Greens Cove for a few days. It was comforting knowing she could count on him at this time. At the end of the hall Paige knocked lightly several times at his door.

A groggy voice called out, but fearing she would rouse the others, Paige didn't answer and instead knocked again. After a moment the door swung open and Kyle, wearing only deep blue pajama bottoms, glared at her.

"Wrong room," he said, "or do I get the treats for the night?"

Stunned by his unexpected assault, Paige reached up to slap his face, but Kyle caught her hand and pulled her into the room and shut the door.

"You're the cruelest man I've ever met, Kyle Buchanan."

"Did you sneak down here and wake me up just to make that announcement?" He switched on the lamp next to his bed.

"Don't be ridiculous."

"Then what is this all about, Paige?"

"Forget it. I'll take care of the situation myself."

He stepped in front of the door. "What situation?"

"Get out of my way," she said, "or I'll scream and wake everybody up."

"Why did you come to my room?" Kyle demanded.

"You have the answer. To offer you 'my treats.' But since you obviously don't want them I'll be on my way." She tried to finesse around him but he blocked her way.

"If you don't let me out of here," she told him, "I'll yell."

Kyle's jaw dropped. "Go ahead," he said. "You're in *my* room. Remember?"

Paige stood her ground. "I've given you fair warning, Kyle, and my composure is fast deteriorating."

"Wait, Paige. Please, please don't have another one of those fits of yours," Kyle said. "Now, calm down and tell me why you've come to see me."

"It was a mistake. I thought this was Nat's room. Excuse me, please."

"I really don't believe that."

"Then don't you think you owe me an apology?"

"Yes. Of course. I'm sorry. I didn't mean to insult you. What I said was totally out of line. Forgive me."

"I accept your apology."

"Now, tell me why you're here."

"Somebody's trying to set fire to something out front."

"What?"

Kyle's dark eyes were skeptical for a moment, then he tore out of the room and down the stairs to the library, where he took a shotgun from the case and began loading it.

"You should have told me this at first," he said. "The house could be burned down by now."

"Kyle, look."

Through the sliding glass doors they could see a small fire blazing under the oak tree. Kyle ran for the doors and Paige followed close behind him.

"Where do you think you're going?" he asked, hesitating for a moment.

"With you."

Momentarily, their eyes locked and held. "Don't you dare take any part of your anatomy over this doorsill," he told her, and slipped into the darkness.

"Be careful," Paige whispered.

She stood slightly behind the draperies of the sliding glass doors and watched as the small fire burned beneath the oak tree. Its bright flickering flames glowed incandescently against the darkness. Hours seemed to pass as Paige waited with bated breath for the black quietness to be shattered with the ring of gunshots, loud voices or the scuffling of a fight. But dead silence prevailed. And in spite of the fact that the night remained dark and still, Paige strained to hear and to see. Finally, in the dim moonlight, she could discern Kyle and Jessie dousing the flames. When the fire was out, they started for the house. Paige ran to the door and held it open for them. "Well, what happened out there?" she asked.

Jessie smiled sheepishly. "I accidentally set fire to my hat, Dr. Avalon," he answered.

"Oh, Jessie, how did you manage that?"

A deep sigh pushed the caretaker's shoulders up and then let them drop carelessly. "I was trying to light my cigar and bent a little too close to my lighter. The brim ignited. When I tried to put it out my slippers started to burn, too. I guess it's a good thing Mr. Kyle came out when he did. Things could have gotten completely out of hand."

Paige stifled a chuckle. "That's a relief," she said. "I thought some madman was trying to put a match to the house."

"I know. I saw you on the balcony and wanted to explain I had started work early because I couldn't sleep. I'm sorry I frightened you."

"All's well that ends well, Jessie," Kyle said, tying the belt of the bathrobe he had slipped on. "Through it all we did find my other two gold coins, which calls for a celebration." He escorted Paige and Jessie to the kitchen and made them a breakfast of blueberries and cream, mushroom omelets, toast and tea.

Afterward, Jessie returned to work and Kyle and Paige, in shorts and sneakers, took an early morning walk around the pond. They were returning to the house when a stretched white Mercedes-Benz limousine pulled into the driveway. Exchanging glances, they started toward it. A slight woman of medium height, dressed in white from head to toe, stepped out of the car.

"Gram!"

"Madame Brandon!"

"Good morning," Andriette Brandon cooed smoothly.

Paige embraced her grandmother. "What are you doing here?" she asked.

"I've come to see you."

"Th-that's terrific," Paige said. "But why didn't you let me know? Why didn't you write? Or call?"

Andriette Brandon looked longingly in the direction of the house. "Are you going to insist that I explain myself while standing out here?" she asked.

"We wouldn't dream of it." Kyle took her by the arm and assisted her across the lawn. "I'm Kyle Buchanan," he said. "I met you many years ago in France while visiting my aunt and uncle, Mary Ann and Nathan Buchanan. It's wonderful seeing you again, Madame Brandon."

Andriette gasped. "Of course," she said. "You're Nathan's nephew. I remember one summer we had some rather wonderful times together."

"Yes. We did."

She paused on the porch and surveyed it carefully. "This is lovely. Let's sit out here." Paige and Kyle waited for Andriette to choose a seat and then sat in chairs on each side of her. "When your mother told me you were working with Nathan and living here in his home, I was thrilled," she told Paige. "I hope he and Mary Ann won't be angry with me for barging in on them like this."

"My aunt died several years ago," Kyle said. "But I'm certain Uncle will be delighted to see you."

His words took Andriette's breath away. "I'm sorry," she said, "Mary Ann was an extraordinary woman."

"Yes," Kyle agreed, "she was."

They talked at length about Europe and Andriette's current concert tour before the older woman directed her attention to her granddaughter. "I saw Steven a few days ago in Paris," she told Paige, "I was shocked by what he had to tell me."

Her words were his cue to leave them and Kyle quickly rose from his chair. "Would you like some tea or a cold drink, Madame Brandon? Paige?"

"No, Kyle, not now." Paige concurred with her grandmother with a shake of her head.

"Then I'll leave you to talk privately," he said going into the house.

Paige met her grandmother's gaze. "I should have written you, Gram, but I knew you would worry."

"Yes, I would have worried, but you should've written anyway."

"What did Steven tell you?" she asked, linking her fingers together and resting her hands in her lap. "Did you come all the way to America because of something he said?"

"Never mind that. What do you have to tell me?"

Paige sighed. "I was wrong, Gram. Steven didn't understand that I need my career. He wanted me to give up everything and go with him to the Middle East."

"If you loved him Paige, how could you let him go so easily?"

"I went through a very difficult period, Gram, and ultimately I got over Steven. I'm satisfied I made the right decision."

"And what will you do, now? Is your work enough to fill your life and make you happy?"

"For the moment."

Andriette got to her feet and went to stand in front of her granddaughter. "If you should ever need me, Paige, please don't hesitate to call or write and let me know. I'm only a plane ride away."

"I know, Gram. And I will. I promise."

Her reunion with Nathan was emotional and happy, and the following morning Andriette Brandon returned to France.

CHAPTER 13

"So, when do you leave for Virginia?" Kyle asked.
"The day after tomorrow."
"I see. Will you be gone long?"
"Approximately two weeks."
"I'm going to miss you, Paige."
She studied him for a moment. "We've all been under an awful lot of pressure lately. Perhaps my going away will be good for everyone."
"I disagree. You and I need to spend more time together. I'd really like to get to know more about you."
"What's puzzling you, Kyle?"
"There's something that I can't put my finger on that's keeping us apart. And I know that once we identify it, everything else will fall into place."
Paige began to stack the dishes on the white-eyelet-skirted table in the corner of the porch. "I'll bet you never thought you'd get the chance to eat a lunch I prepared," she said.
"It was a long time coming."
"Yes, almost three months. I hope you enjoyed it."
She corked the bottle of chablis that rested in the wine cooler.
"Lunch was wonderful."
"Good. Broiled lobster tails and cold asparagus salad were the first dishes my grandmother taught me to cook when I was a little girl and visited her in France."
"She did an excellent job."

"I'm pleased you liked it." She attempted to get to her feet but Kyle caught her hand, encouraging her to remain at the table.

"Paige, don't you feel it, too? Don't you feel that one small something is keeping us off balance?"

"You don't trust me, Kyle."

"It's not that," he replied. "Of course I'd be lying if I said your relationship with Uncle doesn't concern me. But something else is wrong. What is it?"

The sincerity in his eyes caused her to lower her lashes. "I don't know," she said finally. "Perhaps we'll never know."

"But you do admit there's a small something between us that's stifling our relationship."

When Paige met his gaze again she wanted to tell him that the small something he couldn't identify was his uncle's illness. But she couldn't betray Dr. Buchanan's trust. "Yes," she answered, instead.

"Then I'll find out what our little problem is," he said, "and solve it." He got to his feet and picked up the plates and silverware. "I'll help you get these inside." Paige grabbed the glasses and followed him to the kitchen. "By the way, are you going to work this afternoon?"

"No. Nat and I have arrived at an impasse and won't be able to go any further with our work until I return from Virginia." She quickly washed the dishes and Kyle dried them.

"Great. A friend of mine is having an impromptu wedding," he said, looking at his watch, "in about an hour or so. She asked me to give her away. Come with me to Austin, Paige."

"Kyle, how can anyone have an impromptu wedding?"

"Well, my friend finally got this poor guy to say yes," he told her, with an impish smile, "and they made plans to marry in December. But three days ago they decided not to wait, and so today is the big day."

"They must be very much in love."

"Yes. I think they are, and I'm terribly happy for both of them. Say you'll come to Austin with me."

"I'd love to," she said. "It sounds like my kind of wedding."

"I know you'll find it interesting." He checked his watch once again. "All right. It's two-forty, now. I'll meet you on the front porch at three o'clock."

Paige looked aghast. "I can't dress for a wedding in twenty minutes," she said.

"Why not? You're going *to* a wedding. You're not the bride. You shouldn't have anything special to do."

A warm smile curled Paige's lips, for she was relieved to see he was shedding his serious mood. "Whether it's yours or not, Kyle Buchanan, all weddings require special preparations. Nevertheless, I'll see you on the porch at three."

Paige hastily showered, creamed her body, made up her face and brushed her hair, leaving it in loose bouncy waves. She put on a floral mauve-and-apple-green silk crepe de chine wrap dress, high-heeled raisin-purple sandals and her pearls. She took a small quilted matching handbag. At three o'clock she was standing on the front porch admiring Kyle in his steel-gray suit with a navy pinstripe, a white shirt, a navy silk tie and black leather shoes.

"You're beautiful enough to be the bride," Kyle said, taking her hand and leading her across the lawn to his red Ferrari.

"Thank you. You're awfully easy on the eyes yourself. Did you let Nat and Magda know we're leaving?"

"Yes, I told them. Uncle is a little disappointed he's not feeling well enough to come with us."

"He knows your friend?"

"Oh yes. She's really a family friend and very close to Uncle. She'll miss seeing him today."

"Well, Nat has been under a lot of strain lately, Kyle. I hope your friend will understand that."

"I'm sure she will."

In the little white chapel, which sat on a hillside overlooking the lake, Paige admired the sweet-scented fresh flowers and slim ivory-white candles that decorated the aisles and dais. She wondered how Kyle's friend had managed to make such lovely arrangements so quickly and then decided the man she was marrying was no doubt in politics. Politicians had means for getting most things they wanted, Paige told herself.

She turned her attention to the small group of people in the vestry. Many of them she had met at Kyle's Juneteenth party. Remembering the scene she had created there that unforgettable night, Paige hoped no one recognized her.

The soloist performed and the best man and groom joined the minister on the dais. The groom, who looked as if he was in his mid-forties, was tall and lean with silver-gray hair. He was handsome, with an air of success about him.

A couple of bridesmaids and ushers filed down the aisles and then the Wedding March began. When Paige saw the bride on Kyle's arm, she had to grip the back of the pew in front of her to steady herself, the shock was so great. Janet DuBois was beautiful in eggshell-white lace and carrying a bouquet of white orchids entwined with baby's breath.

The ceremony was conventional but brief. Afterward they went across town to the groom's luxurious townhouse for the reception. With the champagne flowing freely, it wasn't long before the house took on a convivial atmosphere. Several hours passed, and at the close of the celebration Kyle and Paige set off for Greens Cove.

"Why didn't you tell me Janet was the family friend that was getting married?" Paige asked, as Kyle skillfully negotiated the curves and hills of the city in the sleek sports car.

"I wanted you to be surprised."

"You accomplished your goal."

"Terrific."

She gave him a sidelong glance. "I'd always thought you and Janet were lovers."

"I know. That's why I wanted you to see, with your own big beautiful brown eyes, exactly what our relationship is and has been for years. Many people have thought otherwise, but we've never been more than just good friends."

"I once overheard her say she'd been trying to convince you that the two of you made a great team. I thought she'd been trying to talk you into marriage."

"That's usually what happens when people eavesdrop. They get all kinds of misinformation."

"Mmm, maybe. Now, tell me, what did she mean?"

"You're a nosy lady, Dr. Paige Avalon."

"Yes, you're right. Talk."

"Janet wanted us to be law partners and for years tried to talk me into opening an office with her."

"She seems to be an excellent lawyer, why didn't you agree to it?"

"Janet's one of the best. But right now I'm more interested in politics than I am in building a law firm."

"Oh? Are you interested in becoming mayor of the city or governor of the state?"

"Neither. I'd like to move into the national arena."

"Mmm, you're going for the gold, huh?"

Kyle laughed. "Yes. Why not?" It was dusk when he pulled into the cobbled driveway. After helping Paige out of the car, he went to the trunk and took out a brown folder. "I've been meaning to ask you about this," he said, handing it to her. "Would you happen to know what it is?"

Paige flipped the cover open and gasped. "It's David Tucker's paper," she said. "Nat and I have been looking for it for weeks. Where did you find it?"

"There, in the trunk of my car. Uncle must have had it in the box that we picked up from his office several weeks ago. It must have slipped out somehow."

"Kyle, this is wonderful. You've just made two people very happy. I'll give this to Nat first thing in the morning."

A light summer wind swirled gently, rustling the leaves of the spreading oak tree as they took seats on the front porch. "Would you like a ride to the airport in the morning?" he asked.

"No, but thanks for offering. I'm going to drive my car and leave it at the airport. That way I won't have to worry about transportation back to Austin when I return. Besides, I have to stop by my apartment before getting my plane."

"Your apartment? Why haven't you ever invited me to that little hideaway of yours?"

"I suppose the opportunity never occurred."

"Seize the moment. Invite me."

Paige smiled. "All right. I'll invite you when I get back."

"Is that a promise?"

"Yes."

"Terrific. I'm going to hold you to it." Cupping Paige's face in his hands, Kyle kissed her tenderly on the lips.

In the library Nathan and Magda sat hand in hand, listening to the cool jazz piano of Andriette Brandon. "It's time to choose, Nathan," Magda said, very much aware of the fact that she was about to force the only man she'd ever loved to make a decision that could possibly break her heart completely.

Dr. Buchanan looked at her curiously. "What do I have to make a choice about?"

"Us."

"What do you mean, Magda?"

"I mean I can't go on like this much longer. I'm beginning to feel unloved and unwanted."

"Magda, why? I love you more today, at this moment, than I ever have in the past."

"Is there another woman in your life, Nathan? Am I sharing you with someone else?"

"I can't understand why you're feeling this way. What have I done to make you so uncertain of my love?"

"It isn't what you've done," Magda said, not telling the whole truth, "it's more a matter of what you haven't done. Nathan, summer's end is fast approaching. Are you planning to send me away?"

"Oh, Magda," he sighed, taking her into his arms, "somehow I've hurt you very deeply. I'm sorry. Tell me

A Toast to Love

what I can do or say to put your mind and heart at ease?"

"Name our wedding day," she told him.

His kiss was fiery, devouring. "Not yet, my love," he whispered. "Not yet."

CHAPTER 14

The research in Virginia had been lengthy, involved and exciting. Paige was able to obtain much valuable information from the local library and historical society in Richmond and secure permission to photograph the several pieces of Lucas Rindleton's handicraft housed in one of the municipal museums. And as luck would have it, while visiting the plantation where he was born, she discovered leads to Virginians who owned some of the antique furniture made by the freedman. But Paige's attempts to follow through on them were quickly aborted. One owner was traveling in Europe and another had recently retired to Mexico. The third and most diligent collector of the craftsman's work simply refused to be interviewed.

Nevertheless, the trip was a success, and Paige made plans for a second junket to Virginia in the fall. And before returning to Austin she again visited Rindleton, Texas, as well as Lucas's descendant in Dallas.

Now, back in her Austin apartment, Paige arranged about the room the several dozen red roses she'd bought for herself. Her thoughts, centered on Greens Cove, tumbled one over the other anxiously. She wouldn't let anyone know she was back in the city, Paige thought. She was much too happy over the success of her research to risk spoiling her mood by subjecting herself to a hostile environment. She'd spend the rest of the weekend in her apartment and celebrate her victory alone. After all, she dreaded seeing Magda again. There was still no clear explanation as to why the woman was angry with her.

Paige finished with the flowers and went to the table where a bottle of champagne was chilling. She filled a fluted goblet and started to the sofa. The doorbell chimed. Startled, Paige froze in her tracks. After a moment the bell chimed once again. Filled with reluctance as well as annoyance Paige crossed the floor and pulled the door open.

Kyle, dressed in white tennis clothes, smiled at her. "My hunch was right," he said. "When did you get back?"

"How did you find my apartment?" Paige asked, her brows knitting with displeasure.

"Aren't you going to invite me inside?"

"Yes, of course. Come in, Kyle." She stood aside and allowed him to ease past her.

"Charming," he said, when he entered the living room. "Very charming, indeed." Slowly he walked around the room and for a second lingered in front of the fireplace studying the painting hanging there. "I've always liked that Chagall," he added, "and if I remember correctly your grandmother is very fond of it, too."

"Yes, she is."

Kyle eyed her casually. "Has my coming here made you terribly unhappy?" he asked.

Avoiding his gaze, Paige focused her attention on the glass clutched in her fidgeting fingers. She wasn't in the mood to face Kyle or the feelings she had for him. She needed more time to be by herself. "No," she lied, "why do you ask?"

"Your expression. You look disappointed that I've come. Are you alone?"

"Of course I'm alone," she answered, an edge to her voice. "And I'm not necessarily disappointed that you've dropped by. Just surprised."

"Good. I'm glad I didn't interrupt anything. I was beginning to think perhaps all these roses had been delivered in person and the delivery man was still lurking about."

"Oh, Kyle, don't be silly," Paige sighed. "I bought the roses myself."

"Why?"

"Simply because I like long-stemmed red roses," she replied.

"I see. They're as lovely as you are."

"Thank you." She glanced at him curiously. "You still haven't told me how you found my apartment."

"The Fletchers gave me your address. I played tennis with them this morning."

"Oh. And how are they?"

"Very well."

Paige drew in her breath and made her way to the opposite side of the room. "Would you like some champagne?" she asked.

"I'd love some," Kyle said, sitting on the sofa. "Champagne and roses," he murmured. "That's quite a heady combination. Are we celebrating something?"

Paige filled a second glass and as he took it from her, she sat down beside him. "Yes, I suppose we are. I'm very pleased with the outcome of my Virginia trip."

"I'm happy for you, Paige," Kyle said. "I'm sure Uncle will be overjoyed to hear the good news."

"Is Nat all right?" she asked.

"Yes, he's fine." His eyes hung on her features for a minute. "I'm sure he missed you if that's what you'd like to know." He raised his glass. "Will you propose a proper toast or shall I?"

A bolt of anger shot through Paige; nevertheless, she kept her emotions reined. "A toast isn't necessary," she said, gulping from her glass and getting to her feet. "I'm going to prepare a light supper. Would you care to join me?"

"I'd like that very much," Kyle said, gripping her arm gently, "but, not until after you've given me an explanation for not drinking a toast with me. This makes the second time you've refused."

She paused and gazed at him coolly. "I don't want to fight with you, Kyle. So let's drop the subject for the present time."

"All right," he agreed, releasing her arm unwillingly, "we'll forget it for now. But, I want you to know that later I expect that explanation." He followed her into the kitchen. "What's for supper?" he asked.

"Salmon."

"Great. What do I get to do?"

"Pour yourself another glass of champagne and work up a hearty appetite."

"You've got it. Those are two things that I'm excellent at."

Kyle's shrewd eyes followed Paige around the kitchen as she prepared their evening meal. She wore no makeup and her hair fell in soft bouncy waves about her face. The long soft blue cotton lounging shift that she wore enhanced her exquisite beauty, and Kyle ached to take her in his arms and hold her close against him. What was it that was keeping them at odds with each other? he wondered. If, and he realized *that* was a big if, she had been telling him the truth all along about her relationship with Nat, why couldn't they resolve their differences and get on with their lives? He had to find out what the problem was that stood between them, and he silently resolved to find out before leaving her that night. "Something smells terrific," he said, teasingly. "I suppose that's another one of your grandmother's recipes."

"No. This happens to be one of my own creations," Paige told him, as she quickly combined chunks of salmon, seasonings and cream with a mixture of sautéed fresh vegetables. After allowing it to simmer several minutes, she stirred in shredded spinach, pasta and Parmesan cheese. She filled their plates, added hot rolls and butter to their fare and took them to the balcony. *"Voilà,"* she said, taking her seat. "I hope you're hungry."

"I'm half starved," Kyle replied, filling their glasses with more champagne.

For a moment Paige held Kyle's gaze. She should tell him about his uncle's illness, she thought, and clear up their misunderstanding once and for all. But would that be fair to Nat? Would he be able to cope with the fact that Kyle knew he was ill? Frankly, she was tired of the lie she was living and wanted to set herself free by telling Kyle the truth. Maybe then, if nothing else, they could at least be friends. Paige drew in her breath and let it out slowly. You're being entirely too selfish, she told herself. Above all else, you must be true to your word.

"This isn't the front porch at Greens Cove," she interrupted their silence, "but it'll just have to do."

"You, your balcony and dinner are all wonderful," Kyle said, looking out at the river and greenery below, "and I'm pleased I was foresightful enough to invite myself over."

Paige smiled. "Perhaps we can have a pleasant evening after all," she said.

"Of course we can." He took her hand in his and squeezed it tenderly. "Tell me, when do you plan to come back to Greens Cove? I hope you don't intend to hide out here, too long."

"Oh, I'm going back on Monday," Paige said. "Hopefully by then I'll feel up to Magda's cold shoulder. By the way, how is she?"

"Magda is fine."

"Did she ever tell you or Nat why she's angry with me?"

Kyle's features clouded. "She hasn't said anything to me."

"I wish I could find out what I've done or said to offend her."

They finished their dinner, cleared the table and returned to the living room. During that time Kyle was quiet, deep in thought. As they settled themselves on the sofa, he asked, "When did you first notice Magda's change in attitude?"

"After my first trips to Dallas and Rindleton."

"Perhaps," Kyle spoke hesitantly, "Magda's angry with you because of something I told her."

"What do you mean?"

"Well, while you were away Magda and I had a long talk about a number of things including Uncle."

A smile curled on Paige's lips as she prepared herself to hear that Kyle had learned of his uncle's illness and love for Magda Winslow. "Before you tell me what you may have said to anger her, I want to hear what Magda told you about Nat."

"I guess nothing of importance," Kyle said, watching her closely. "I don't remember any specifics."

Paige's expectant expression faded as she realized Kyle hadn't yet learned of the secrets in his uncle's personal life. Then, why did he seem so pensive and serious? "All right. What were you going to tell me?" "Only that Magda seemed terribly agitated when I told her I suspected you were trying to seduce and marry Uncle in order to advance your career." Paige's jaw dropped, and for a moment she was speechless. "Why would you do such a thing? No wonder the woman is angry with me. Do you know what you've done, Kyle? Do you realize how much you've hurt Magda?"

"Look, Paige, you've known all along how I feel about your relationship with Uncle. Why are you getting so upset?"

"I'm upset, Kyle Buchanan, because you've lied. And that lie has not only hurt me but it has hurt Magda very deeply."

"I didn't lie, Paige. I voiced my suspicions."

"And your suspicions have caused us all a great deal of unnecessary pain."

"I'm still not convinced my feelings are incorrect."

"Oh, I see. Well, I have some information that'll do just that."

"I'd love to hear it." Paige opened her mouth to speak, then immediately closed it, for she thought of the promises she'd made to Nathan Buchanan on so many occasions. She realized that if she told the truth at this time, probably, he would neither forgive nor trust her again. But what choices did she have? As things stood all of their lives had been made unhappy because of those terrible secrets. Now, Paige had the opportunity to put the dreadful situation aright. She would explain everything to Kyle and hope for Nat's forgive-

ness. "You seem to be at a loss for words," Kyle said.
"Why don't you drink another glass of champagne and
get your thoughts flowing again."

"No. I'm afraid champagne won't help at all. I'm
about to betray a trust, Kyle, and I hope with all my
heart I'm forgiven."

"If what you're going to say is the truth and will clear
up all of this, I'm certain you will be forgiven. And more
than anything I want to hear that my suspicions have
been unfounded."

"They're unfounded, Kyle. Nathan and Magda are
very much in love, and earlier this year had planned to
marry." Paige sighed audibly and looked at him.
"Didn't you have any idea of what was going on?"

"No, I didn't." His tone was cold and he gazed at her
with disbelieving eyes. "What broke them up? You?"

She shook her head. "The culprit was essential blepharospasm."

"What the heck is that, Paige?"

"A disease that Nathan has contracted. Unexpectedly
and uncontrollably his eyes slam shut and can't be
opened again for several minutes." Kyle looked as
though he would faint and Paige quickly took ice from
the wine cooler and rubbed it gently across his forehead. "Are you all right?" she asked.

"I don't know." He eased to the edge of the sofa and
dropped his head in his hands. "Paige, I didn't know
about any of this. Why didn't Magda or Uncle tell me?"

"You and your uncle are very protective of each
other, Kyle. He didn't want to worry you."

"Uncle should have told me," he whispered.

"Yes, I agree. I tried to convince him of that any
number of times, especially after we had the car accident, but he wouldn't hear of it."

"Can he be cured?"

"Nat has tried a number of treatments, but nothing has worked so far. Perhaps, somehow, you can persuade him to see a doctor who can help him. Of course, the only thing he's ever allowed me to do was console him occasionally after one of his attacks."

"And all this time I thought you were trying to—"

"Yes."

"I'm sorry, Paige. Forgive me. Please."

"I forgive you, Kyle. But what am I to do about Nat and Magda? On top of everything else, she now thinks I want to marry the man she loves. And I've broken my promise to Nathan."

"You had no choice," he said. "I was making a terrible mess of things. But don't worry, I'll speak with both of them on Monday."

"Why wait until Monday?" Paige searched his face. "Why not talk with them tonight or tomorrow?"

"They're not at Greens Cove," he said. "Magda and Uncle have been in Houston for the past several days."

A surge of optimism rushed through Paige. "Hopefully, they've gone to the medical center to have one of the doctors there examine Nat." She smiled. "Then, Monday will have to be the day. I'm afraid your uncle is going to be terribly angry with me for upsetting you. He may not allow me back in his home."

"I promise," Kyle said, raising his right hand, "you'll be forgiven and everything will be under control when you arrive on Monday."

"I do hope I've done the right thing."

"Believe me, Paige, you have. I can assure you that I'll do everything in my power to help Uncle find a cure for his illness."

"I know you will." She lowered her lashes and was

thoughtful for a moment before speaking again. "Tell me, Kyle, would you object to Nathan marrying again?"

"Although you may think the contrary," Kyle said, taking both Paige's hands in his, "I'm not a heartless man. I love my uncle and want him to be happy. And if he should decide to marry Magda, my blessings are guaranteed. Besides, I like her and think she'll make Uncle a wonderful wife."

"I'm relieved to hear that."

He kissed her fingertips lightly. "Now. What about us? Has Uncle's illness been the one thing that's kept us off balance?"

"Yes. I think so."

"All right. We'll know for certain soon enough. There's one other thing that I'd like you to explain to me tonight."

"What's that?"

"Why you've consistently refused to drink a toast with me." She tried to free her fingers from his grasp, but he refused to release them. "I want an answer," he said.

As Kyle's warm strong fingers gently caressed her palms, Paige closed her eyes and clenched her teeth together in an effort to control her emotions. "I guess my pride wouldn't allow it," she replied, at last. "I couldn't bring myself to drink to your salutations when I knew you didn't mean them. You've had some rather awful thoughts about me, Kyle."

"That's true. But I've had some very wonderful ones about you, too." His lips brushed her eyelids and then her nose. "Things are going to be different with us from now on," he said. "Just wait. You'll see."

"I hope so," Paige whispered. She dissolved in his arms as his lips claimed hers in a lingering fevered kiss.

CHAPTER 15

Her shoulders were bared in the simple white sundress she wore, and the early morning breeze was dry and cool. Nevertheless, Paige's body had been dampened by a light film of perspiration. Even the soles of her feet were moist and slipped about uncomfortably in her high-heeled taupe leather sandals. At a stop sign she abruptly brought her metallic blue-gray Porsche to a standstill, took a handkerchief from her handbag and dried her hands as well as the moist steering wheel. Afterward, she continued her drive. She told herself she had to stop worrying. She had to stop feeling guilty for telling Kyle about Magda and Nathan. After all, it was the right thing to do. So why did she feel like a criminal? "You've violated a confidence, and now you must pay the price." She spoke the words aloud.

Paige tried to console herself, realizing she couldn't walk into the mansion at Greens Cove looking and feeling like a transgressor. She attempted to focus her attention on the scenery, but couldn't concentrate on the green hills or the winding silvery river. She made an effort to review her new research material and failed miserably. Her thoughts continuously returned to Kyle, Nathan and Magda.

Finally, Paige gave herself the best lecture she'd been able to come up with all morning. There's really no need to worry, she thought. Kyle promised to talk with both Nathan and Magda. All will go well. Have courage. She turned onto the cobbled drive and was comforted by the sight of Kyle's red Ferrari parked in front of the garage. Smiling, she pulled up beside it, got out of her car and headed for the house.

Magda walked out on the porch and folded her arms in front of her. She's been waiting for me, Paige thought. She's anxious to make amends. Wearing her bright smile more comfortably now, Paige waved and hastened her steps.

"Good morning, Magda. How was your trip to Houston?"

"I never dreamed you'd go this far, Paige," Magda said, her tone hostile.

Startled, Paige felt her legs weaken, and she leaned against the porch railing to support herself. "Have you spoken with Kyle this morning?" she asked.

"No, I haven't. He's been too busy arguing with his uncle. And from what I've been able to gather you're the cause of it all."

Paige sighed and stared at the pastel-colored cotton rug that covered a small portion of the porch in front of the white wicker sofa. "Magda, I had to tell Kyle about Nat's illness. He was on the verge of destroying all our lives because of it."

"And just how was he about to do that?"

"He wrecked our friendship, Magda. He thought I wanted to marry Nathan."

"And you don't?" Magda asked, studying her closely.

"No. I've told you that once. I thought you believed me."

"I did, then."

"And now?"

"Now I believe Kyle."

"Magda, don't you see that Kyle misunderstood my

relationship with Nathan because on several occasions he saw me consoling him after one of his attacks? He thought I was making love to his uncle when I was only trying to comfort him."

Magda looked as if someone had thrown cold water in her face. Slowly, she eased down on the sofa, her gaze frozen on Paige. "Then, Kyle was wrong?"

"Yes, Magda. I want Nathan to be my friend. That's all. Kyle made a mistake."

"Paige, I don't know what to say. I'm so very embarrassed."

"You don't have to say anything. It's all over. Please let's forget it."

"No. No, I can't pretend nothing has happened. I've done and said some terrible things to you, Paige, and I'm sorry. Do you think we can ever be friends again?"

"Magda, I've been wishing with all my heart you'd want that," Paige said, embracing her and sighing with relief. "I'm so happy we've finally straightened everything out."

"I am, too." Magda smiled.

"Now, tell me about Houston. Did you find a doctor who can help Nat?"

Slipping her hands into the pockets of her yellow silk dress, Magda got to her feet and moved to the edge of the porch. The happiness that had filled her eyes slowly began to ebb. "The doctor we saw, Paige, could only recommend the same treatment Nat is taking now. He wasn't able to give us any new hope."

"Oh no," Paige breathed softly. She rose from the sofa and went to stand next to Magda. "Don't lose faith," she said. "I know Nat will be cured. And soon."

"I do hope you're right," Magda replied.

Nathan Buchanan rushed angrily out of the house

and halfway down the steps before spotting Paige and Magda at the far end of the porch. Fixing them with a cold steady gaze, he retraced his steps and went to stand before them. His breathing was deep, rapid. His eyes reflected his wrath. Paige had never before seen the historian so angry, and it saddened her as she realized she was the cause of his profound unhappiness.

"Nathan, please calm down," Magda said. "Surely all of this has happened for the best."

"Stay out of this, Magda." He spoke the words so softly that it frightened them. "Why did you do it, Paige? What will you possibly gain by explaining my affairs to my nephew?"

Because Paige couldn't bear to meet Nathan's gaze, she turned her attention to the colorful summer flowers that bordered the walkway. Her worst fears had materialized. The historian was furious with her. And she was feeling terribly guilty. "I'm sorry I've hurt and disappointed you, Nathan. But Kyle had to be told. He had become awfully confused by our relationship."

"Our relationship?"

"Yes. He thought we were lovers. Didn't he tell you?"

Nathan's anger began to subside, and he felt as though the rug had been pulled out from under him, leaving him unsteady, stunned. "He mentioned no such thing to me."

"But it's true, Nathan," Magda said. "He spoke to me about his suspicions several weeks ago, and I'm ashamed to say I believed him."

"Magda, how could you?" His tone revealed the deep hurt her words had caused him.

Nathan sank onto the sofa and Magda sat down beside him. Tenderly, she covered his hands with her own. They felt cold. Lifeless. "I feel awful about it, Nathan, but I doubted you."

His face, that only seconds earlier had been contorted with anger and then pain, was now emotionless. For a long time he neither moved nor spoke, but remained sitting, like a beautiful bronze statue, deep in thought. When at last he came out of his reverie, his fingers had grown warm and strong again. He gripped Magda's hands firmly and looked into her eyes. "I suppose it was only natural for my deceitfulness to come to such an end," he said. "I never should have tried to hide my illness. Not only have I hurt Kyle, but I've also hurt you and Paige. Forgive me."

"Of course I forgive you, Nathan," Magda said, smiling and kissing him gently.

He got to his feet and held out his hand to Paige. She slipped her fingers into it. "I burdened you much too long with my problems," he told her. "I hope somehow you'll find a way to excuse my selfishness."

"I harbor no resentments, Nathan," Paige said. "Your friendship will always be precious to me."

"Uncle, I have very good news," Kyle said, walking out on the porch. His eyes briefly met Paige's and then shifted to Magda and Nathan. "I didn't know you would get here so early, Paige," he told her. "I haven't had a chance to speak with Magda yet."

"We've all talked, Kyle," Nathan said, "and I think we've managed to forgive each other. Nevertheless, I suppose I owe you an explanation regarding my relationship with Paige. She and I are not having an affair. I regret you were led to believe the contrary."

"Yes, Uncle, I know that now."

"But, I think you should know that Magda and I did at

one time consider marriage. Now, however, it's out of the question."

"Why?" Kyle asked.

"Because of my illness, of course. I can't risk becoming a burden to Magda."

Tears sprang to Magda's eyes and she quickly turned away from her companions, attempting to hide the pain Nathan's words caused her. How she wished she could convince him that no matter what his problems, she could never see him as a burden. She loved him too much.

"That's exactly what I came out here to talk with you about," Kyle said. "I've just spoken with a friend of mine in Houston, and he's found a doctor who can help you."

"This fast?" Nathan asked.

A sheepish smile curled Kyle's lips. "I called him after Paige and I talked Friday night," he said, "and he promised to check out a few leads for me over the weekend. He's friends with several of the doctors at his tennis club, and a couple of them know all about essential blepharospasm. It seems it can be cured with a simple operation."

Magda gasped and embraced Nathan. "Our prayers have been answered," she told him, her eyes overflowing with tears of joy. "Oh, Nat, I'm so very happy for you. For us."

"That terrific news will change all our lives, Kyle," Paige said. "I did do the right thing by breaking my promises to Nat, didn't I?"

Kyle smiled and brushed her cheek with his index finger. "Yes, you did," he answered.

They rejoiced in the good news and failed to notice Nathan did not share their optimism. Worry lines deeply creased his handsome face, as he stood with his arm draped loosely around Magda's waist, staring into the distance. "Your friend's solution to my problem sounds a little too simplistic for me," Nathan announced. "Are there no risks involved? No chance for failure?" Their smiles and tears of joy quickly faded as Nathan's somber words penetrated their consciousness. "I think before we do any more celebrating we should get additional information on the procedure and the success rates the doctors have had with it."

"Did he mention anything like that?" Magda asked anxiously.

Kyle sighed and slumped against the railing. "No risks were mentioned," he said, "though I suppose there must be some for certain patients. He did tell me, however, that the doctors have achieved an 80 percent cure rate without recurrence. And for most of those who suffered recurrence, a second operation often cured them."

They exchanged troubled glances. "I still think your chances for being cured are excellent, Nathan," Paige said. She returned her attention to Kyle. "Did you find out the cause of essential blepharospasm or any details about the surgery?"

"The exact cause is not known," Kyle answered. "But doctors tend to believe it stems from erratic signals from the brain that short-circuit the nerves and muscles that open and close the eyelids. The surgical treatment involves removing part of the nerve system that controls the lids."

There was silence on the porch for several minutes before Magda ventured to speak. "Please, Nathan, try it," she said, "not just for yourself, but for us, too."

"I agree with Magda, Uncle," Kyle added quickly.

Slowly, Nathan Buchanan covered his face with his hands and everyone present realized he had lost control of his eyelids. "All right," he said, at last. "I'll see what your doctor has to say."

The two weeks that followed Nathan's critical decision were spent in consultations and examinations. And when the time finally arrived for him to undergo surgery, Magda, Kyle and Paige were at the hospital. The operation was lengthy but simple. And the pronouncement that the historian was at last cured filled them with relief and happiness. While Magda and Kyle remained in Houston with Nathan, Paige returned to her Austin apartment where she worked diligently on the Rindleton Project.

It was late afternoon when the postman arrived and Paige stopped work to read her mail. She promptly put her Bloomingdale's statement aside unopened and read the letter from her mother. Her parents were just back from a two-week holiday in the Orient, and the anecdotes that Mrs. Avalon related to her daughter about their trip made her laugh as well as feel a little homesick and lonely. After reading the letter twice Paige stuck it on the desk, in anticipation of enjoying it a third time before getting back to work, and picked up a small gray envelope with unfamiliar handwriting. Tearing it open, her eyes immediately searched for a signature. It was signed Kyle. Paige read the brief message and smiled. He was inviting her to a formal dinner at Greens Cove.

Paige read the note once again paying close attention to the date and time—Thursday evening, September 27, 7 P.M. She checked the clock on the dashboard of the Porsche. It was five minutes before seven. So, where were all the other guests? Feeling a little uncomfortable and confused, she got out of her car and crossed the lawn.

Paige hadn't been to Greens Cove in weeks, and as she climbed the steps of the spacious gray-painted porch she was smitten by a wave of nostalgia. She remembered the happiness and excitement she had felt meeting Nathan and moving into the stately old mansion. She remembered the joy she'd experienced as she began work on the Rindleton Project. And never would she forget how handsome Kyle had looked the time she watched him through the binoculars exercising under the oak tree. Those first spring days in the rolling green hills of Austin had been wonderful. Paige pressed the doorbell and waited.

Startled because she expected to see Kyle, Paige stared at the woman in the black-and-white maid's uniform who held the door open for her. "Mrs. Stone . . . I'm . . . uh . . . I've come . . ."

"I know, Miss Avalon. Mr. Buchanan is waiting for you in the dining room. Come in." Paige followed Kyle's housekeeper down the hall as though she'd never been in the house before. "You look very beautiful," Mrs. Stone said.

Paige smiled. "Thank you."

Mrs. Stone stepped aside, allowing Paige to enter the room that was filled to capacity with long-stemmed red roses in crystal vases and wicker baskets. The sweet fragrance of the flowers filled the area and complemented the soft glow of several white candles burning in long silver holders. At the far end of the room was a fountain flowing with champagne. Kyle Buchanan, gorgeous in black tie, stood next to it.

"Hello, Kyle." She hadn't intended it, but her words came out in a whisper.

"Paige." His voice ignited the flame deep within her that burned only for him. Slowly and deliberately, he devoured her beauty. Her hair was exactly as he liked it, curled and loose about her shoulders. Her deep green matte-jersey dress molded itself delicately to her body, and its long sleeves and cascading silk-organza ruffles down one side gave it an added touch of elegance. She wore high-heeled silver sandals and a brushed silver handbag hung from her shoulder. "You look exquisite, as always," Kyle told her.

"I was afraid I had come on the wrong day," she said. "No one else has arrived."

"And no one else will." He held out his hand and she crossed the room to him. "You're my only guest."

"I see."

"So, how do you like the little touches I've added to the room?" he asked.

"The roses?"

"And the champagne."

"I like them very much. But, of course, you knew I would."

"Yes, I knew." He eased two fluted crystal goblets under the flow of wine and after filling them handed one to Paige. "Shall we drink a toast?" he asked.

"Yes," she whispered.

"Will you propose it or shall I?"

"You."

For a long time he held her gaze and then softly said, "To love."

"To love," she repeated, as they touched their glasses and drank quickly.

Kyle smiled, kissed her lightly on the lips and raised   **N47** his glass the second time. She blindly followed his example. "To you," he said, "the one and only woman I have and will ever love." Paige's breath caught in her throat and she searched his face anxiously. "Be my wife, Paige," he whispered, holding her close to him.

"Oh, Kyle, yes," she whispered. "Yes."

The housekeeper deliberately rattled the china she held in her hands. "Would you like dinner served, now, Mr. Buchanan?" she asked.

"No, no, Mrs. Stone," Kyle answered. "We'll have dinner later. Much, much later." He put their glasses aside and once again enfolded Paige in his arms. "You're the most wonderful person I've ever known, and I love you," he whispered.

Paige gazed into his eyes and knew he had meant every word he had spoken. "I love you," she replied.

That September night, Kyle and Paige toasted many things before having a very late dinner. A very late dinner indeed.